Other books by Brian Doyle

THE LOW LIFE

UNCLE RONALD

SPUD IN WINTER

SPUD SWEETGRASS

COVERED BRIDGE

EASY AVENUE

ANGEL SQUARE

UP TO LOW

YOU CAN PICK ME UP AT PEGGY'S COVE

HEY, DAD!

Mary Ann Alice

Mary Ann Alice

...

BRIAN DOYLE

A GROUNDWOOD BOOK
DOUGLAS & McINTYRE VANCOUVER TORONTO BUFFALO

Copyright © 2001 by Brian Doyle
First published in the USA in 2002
Second paperback printing 2002

All rights reserved. No part of this book may be reproduced, stored in a
retrieval system or transmitted in any form or by any means, without the
prior written permission of the publisher or, in the case of photocopying or
other reprographic copying, a licence from CANCOPY (Canadian
Reprography Collective), Toronto, Ontario.

Groundwood Books / Douglas & McIntyre Ltd.
720 Bathurst Street, Suite 500, Toronto, Ontario M5S 2R4

Distributed in the USA by Publishers Group West
1700 Fourth Street, Berkeley, CA 94710

We acknowledge the financial support of the Canada Council for the Arts,
the Ontario Arts Council and the Government of Canada through the Book
Publishing Industry Development Program for our publishing activities.

ONTARIO ARTS COUNCIL
CONSEIL DES ARTS DE L'ONTARIO

National Library of Canada
Cataloguing in Publication Data
Doyle, Brian
Mary Ann Alice
ISBN 0-88899-453-2 (bound). —ISBN 0-88899-454-0 (pbk.)
I. Title.
PS8557.O87M37 2001   jC813'.54   C2001-900901-1
PZ7.D69Ma 2001

Design by Michael Solomon
Cover illustration by Ted Nasmith
Printed and bound in Canada

Let this book be dedicated to Sandy Farquharson

TABLE OF CONTENTS

PART I

1

The Bell and the Falls

M Y name is Mary Ann Alice. Mary Ann Alice McCrank.

I was named after the bell in the steeple of St. Martin's Church in Martindale. They got the bell and named it back in 1885. They named it Mary Ann Alice. That was almost forty-one years ago. Seems like a long time. But my mother says it's not a long time.

My mother, Fuzzy McCrank, is forty-one years old, too.

She says if I say forty-one years is a long time one more time she won't finish the dress she's making me for the next big covered-bridge dance at Low if there is one.

I love that bell in St. Martin's steeple. The sound of it.

When my father, Frank McCrank, pulls the rope on Sundays and special days or weddings or funerals, you can hear the pretty sound of the bell all up and down the Gatineau River, down to Low and up to Venosta and all along the tumbling farms. And everybody hears it but not very many people know I'm named after it and what it's saying when it rings. Mary Ann Alice...Mary Ann Alice...

I'm quite poetic, I don't mind saying.

My teacher, Patchy Drizzle, says I've the soul of a poet.

He wrote that on a story I handed in to him last spring. I asked him would he not say that in front of the others because they'd tease me and he said he wouldn't.

I told my mother, though. About having a poetic soul.

She had a sad look on her for a minute and then it went away and she said, "Well, the soul of a poet or not, get yer pail and get out there. There's poetic cows to be milked and they're waitin' on ya!"

I told my father. My father, too, is poetic.

My father, when he feels poetic, he brings out his bugle and he walks down the river to the Paugan Falls— you have to go for about two little valleys to get there— and he plays his bugle to the thundering water there and you can hardly hear him the thunder of the water is so thunderous!

But it's quiet up here at our farm. You don't really hear the roar of the falls. But it's there.

You don't hear it but you do.

The way you listen to your heart at night in bed.

If you want to hear your heart, you can. But if you don't, well then just go on ahead and go to sleep and forget about it.

But the pretty church bell from St. Martin's you can hear.

Mary Ann Alice...Mary Ann Alice...

Sometimes it's carefree and happy like on Easter Sunday or for weddings and sometimes sad and muffled when somebody dies.

And something else you hear these days. Something not so easy to understand. It's the rumors.

Everybody's talking about something frightening and exciting. Somebody's going to build a dam. Right here.

And the falls will disappear.

Can you imagine it? It doesn't seem believable!

How could it be possible? That falls like the Paugan Falls would just disappear? But that's what's going to happen, they say. And I'm very worried about it.

And another thing. The whole river's going to come up. The water will rise up. How far up will it come? Everybody says different. Some say it won't come up much at all. Others say it will come up to your front door.

Others say—those who read the Bible all the time— that they're going to build themselves an ark like Noah did, and get in it and wait.

Eddy Lamarr says he's going to build an ark up on top of Dizzy Peak, which is on his land. His wife, Lizzie, says he can build it all he wants but she'll never get in it. My father, Frank McCrank, says it's just like in the Bible. Noah in the Bible had a terrible time trying to get his wife, Mrs. Noah, to get in and sit in his ark. My father says Noah and what's her name his wife hated each other because they both snored in their sleep. How he knows this is beyond me. I think he's only pulling my leg.

My father likes to joke and tease. Lots of people who

like to joke and tease only do it to cover up how they're not very smart themselves. But my father does it because he likes you. And he's very smart as well as being poetic. He studied engineering for a while before he came up the Gatineau to become a farmer.

He's worried about the river rising, too.

2

Developments

TODAY'S the day of the big church picnic. Father Foley says it's the last church picnic that will ever be held here at the falls. All this'll be under cement in a few months.

Everybody's here and there's so much to think about while I'm helping with the supper.

The tables underneath the trees are bending with the weight of what's to eat. There's bees and wasps and butterflies and small birds fluttering over the food.

And there's Mickey McGuire Jr. over there working on the firewood for the stew pot hanging there.

I'm going to kiss Mickey McGuire Jr. one day. I don't know when, but I'm going to kiss him.

There's small white clouds in the blue sky. I'm excited but I don't know why. Something's going to happen but I don't know what. And I almost feel afraid. Patchy, my teacher, says poets always feel that way. Excited and sort of afraid.

So much to think about. The heat bugs are singing.

There's grasshoppers arching. You can sidespy them in the tall grass around and about the upper field.

Oh, another thing I should tell you. I'm developing very quick, or so my mother says. My father started for a while calling me Sprout. I told him to stop it and he did. My father's a joker like I told you but he never goes too far. He knows when to quit, not like some around here.

Like the ferryman, Fitzpatrick, down the river below the falls at Fitzpatrick's Ferry. Sometimes if he's dropping off a passenger on a real dark night and the passenger is drunk Fitzpatrick'll pull up not quite to the shore and yell, "All right, we're here. Step off!" And of course the passenger steps off and falls into the water up to his neck. It's usually Boiled Head McCooey who falls for it.

Now, that's not funny.

Poor Boiled Head. His head is so boiled he doesn't know where he is half the time. Everybody says it's because he was in World War I but never mind any of that.

Now that I'm developing, my mother gets me to bind myself ever since I told her I get a bit sore after scrubbing the floor or square dancing like I did this summer when I got to go to the dance at Low and danced with Mickey McGuire Jr. the whole night.

My mother sewed me a hem on a white strip off a sheet and I wrapped myself and she tied it at the back. While she was tying it I told her I felt like kissing Mickey McGuire Jr. the other day while we were walking through the covered bridge.

I told her I'd tell Father Foley the new young priest from Farrellton about me and Mickey Jr. and the covered bridge in my next confession, and she said never mind telling him anything about the likes of that. What you do in that regard, she said, is your own business. Father Foley is busy enough, she said, without me bothering him with stories about things I'm only thinking of doing and haven't even done yet. And even if I did kiss Mickey McGuire Jr. in the covered bridge or let him kiss me in some future time, it would be none of Father Foley's business anyway. She said priests know far too much about people's private life as it is.

They often say around here that my mother is sometimes, what you call, outspoken.

Now I don't have to get my mother to tie me at the back with the strip of sheet anymore. I leave the knot in and I get the strip off by slipping it down and stepping out of it. To put it back on I just step into it and wriggle it back up until I'm in it.

It feels good being wrapped like that. I don't get so sore anymore after cutting wood or churning butter or rowing the boat.

And I'm wondering if Mickey McGuire Jr. and I will be walking through the covered bridge again sometime soon.

Mickey McGuire Jr. is Ronnie O'Rourke's great-nephew. Mickey Jr.'s father came to live with Ronnie O'Rourke when he was about my age.

He escaped here with Gramma Nora, who is Great-uncle Ronald's sister. That was after her husband, who was also called Mickey McGuire, stole Great-uncle Ronnie's horse, Second Chance Lance, and ran into the train.

Maybe you heard about that. It's very complicated, like everything else around here.

Then Great-uncle Ronnie married Cecelia Hickey in a big Thanksgiving Day wedding and now they have seven kids. Mickey Jr.'s father, Mickey Sr., grew up and married Martha McCooey, daughter of old Boner McCooey and they had Mickey Jr., who's about my age now and who walked me through the covered bridge when the whip-poorwill was singing so many bright tunes that your ears would get painful just listening to all of it.

But never mind all that. You'll never be able to keep it straight anyway so just forget I ever tried to explain it in the first place.

In the covered bridge we stopped for a minute and leaned on the rail and looked down into the water of Stag Creek rushing down toward the Gatineau River and we listened to the whippoorwill.

Mickey dropped a small stick into the creek. He said that stick was now free to go anywhere in the world. Down Stag Creek into the waters of the Gatineau River and on down to the Ottawa River. Then into the St. Lawrence River and then into the Atlantic Ocean. From there the lit-tle stick, Mickey said, would go anywhere the wind would take it and the currents. Africa, India, Australia, China...

It was around then that I felt like kissing him.

And I also felt like writing about it.

It was the same kind of feeling. Kissing him and writing about kissing him.

I wonder what's going to happen in the future? Will I get married? Or will I be a poet? I think I'll be a poet.

A girl poet. The first one!

3

The Best Stew

ICKEY McGuire Jr.'s grandfather was killed by the Gatineau train. My father, Frank McCrank, told me all about it. He was there and saw the whole thing. The train wheels ran over that man so many times that he was cut up into chunks the size of stewing meat. My father was a soldier at the Battle of Brennan's Hill. He was a bugler. He came here with the soldiers that time when they came to collect the taxes. He got the soldiers up in the morning with his bugle. He liked it so much up around here that when he got older he came up here and started to be a farmer.

And married my mother who is also a McCrank, but not the same family of McCranks but never mind that.

There's a huge black iron pot of stew set up near where Mickey Jr. is working on the wood. It's simmering away, hanging over red-hot burning hardwood knots. Every now and then Mrs. Kealey comes over with a long wood spoon and stirs the stew. She's in charge. She makes the best stew on the whole Gatineau River. She's a widow. They say her husband died because he ate too much. Probably he ate stew mostly, because her stew is the very best.

My father, Frank McCrank, said that Mr. Kealey's last wish was to have the grave hole he'd be buried in filled with gravy and vegetables so's he'd feel right at home.

That's not true, of course, not a word of it.

Here at the picnic, when Mrs. Kealey stirs the stew, the carrots and potatoes and onions and mushrooms and peas swim up to the top of the brown gravy and make you so hungry your mouth starts to water up.

Also rolling up in the dark brown gravy in the big iron pot when Mrs. Kealey stirs are chunks of stewing meat the size of chunks of stewing meat.

Oh, I can't help but think, standing over the pot and looking in, of Mickey McGuire Jr.'s grandfather, old Mickey McGuire himself, how the train cut him up into chunks like that! Other people look in the stew pot and they think of stew. But not me.

How hard it is, sometimes, to have the soul of a poet!

4

What Mean Hughie Did

THERE'S hundreds here at the picnic.

And there's lots to do. Babies are asleep in baskets in the shade of the trees and covered over with cheesecloth for the flies or crying or sucking in their mothers' arms or bouncing like rubber dolls on their fathers' knees. The kids are chasing in and out or fooling around down by the water throwing rocks into the foam from the falls or yelling and playing hide-and-seek or kick-the-can. Some of the older boys are diving into the whirlpools and trying to swim to the other side without getting carried down to the calmer water below. Or they're riding the big pine logs out there, riding them like wild horses.

Most of the girls and women are helping with the food and the baking and the knitting and the sewing shows that are spread out along the long tables. Biscuits, bread, pies, cakes, custards, baked apples and sweets and beans and shawls and socks and quilts.

The men are standing around, dressed up, smoking in little circles or they have their suit jackets off and are playing baseball or horseshoes or twisting wrists in the hot September sun.

The older men and the old men are smoking their pipes in their Sunday cuffs and straw hats and sitting on stools and kitchen chairs brought from home amongst the babies in the baskets under the trees with butterflies butterflying in and out around them.

And the older ladies and the old ladies are in their chairs under the umbrellas and under the big tent at the bingo tables out of the sun.

And there's the O'Malley girls, the old twins, Edith and Mildred under their canopy. They're talking there with Great-uncle Ronald and my father, Frank, and Mickey McGuire Jr.'s Gramma Nora and His Honor the Mayor of Low, Even Steven.

They're talking about something funny that happened on the farm next to theirs up the river an hour or so by rowboat, up past St. Martin's Church and her bell, Mary Ann Alice. The farm belongs to their neighbor Mean Hughie and what they're talking about is binder twine and what Mean Hughie did to a lawyer who made the mistake of going into Mean Hughie's house and telling him something about what's going to happen when the dam is built.

"Mean Hughie tied a lawyer up and laid him on the sawhorse. He tied him up tight with binder twine," says one of the old O'Malley girls, the identical twins whichever one it is nobody can tell.

Then Great-uncle Ronald says it was more like he *rolled* the lawyer up in binder twine much the way a spider would roll up a fly in spider web. Then Mayor Even Steven says no, no, he *wrapped* the lawyer, Mean Hughie wrapped the lawyer with binder twine the way you'd tie up a roast of beef with cord. And then the other O'Malley girl says no, it was more like Mean Hughie spun the lawyer in binder twine the way a caterpillar would be spun in a cocoon but then, of course, he didn't exactly emerge as a butterfly a little later. Then Gramma Nora says that the lawyer was fortunate that he emerged at all after Mean Hughie was finished with him. This she says out of the side of her mouth.

"If they took all the binder twine in the world and wrapped up all the lawyers in the world, the lawyers would still find a way to steal the money right out of the pockets of your pants while you were standing there looking the other way!" my father, Frank McCrank, says, and everybody agrees.

A binder is a big cutter that a good team of strong horses pulls through a field of grain. The knives of the binder slice back and forward like scissors and cut down the tall grain plants. The grain plants fall on a canvas that moves and then get pushed up tight into a slot and then iron fingers tie up the plants into a bundle with binder twine.

Then the bundle which is called a sheaf is shot out of the binder onto the ground.

Each sheaf of grain is about the size of a pretty little girl.

A little girl with crazy hair and a belt of binder twine around her waist. My father said one time I looked as pretty as a sheaf of grain. I liked it when he said that. Every time I see a sheaf of grain now I think of—guess who? Me!

When the field is completely cut there are hundreds of sheaves, a whole lot of small groups of little girls, lying around all over the field.

Then what they do is the boss sends out kids like me or maybe a little older to pick up the sheaves and stand them up leaning in against each other with their heads together.

This takes all day and it's very tiresome and people usually hate doing it which is why they send us kids out to do it.

Each pyramid should have six or eight sheaves in it. The pyramids are called stooks. There would be dozens and dozens of these stooks in perfect rows in the field when we are finally done.

Dozens of small groups of little girls, their heads together, sharing secrets about what will happen when the river comes up.

The stooks stay that way for a couple of weeks to dry out. Even if it rains the water will drip off the little girls' crazy hair and then it will soon blow dry in the breeze.

There is always plenty of binder twine left over after all this. There's balls of it hanging on nails in the machine shed and rolling around the floor of the granary. It's used for lots of things besides tying up sheaves of grain.

My father always uses binder twine to fix Mayor Even Steven's car.

If a gate is hanging loose you can fix it with binder twine. If the gas wringer washer is broke you can fix it with binder twine. You can mend harness with binder twine. Halter a horse. Fix the handle of the butter churn. Put the wheel back on the wheelbarrow. You can tie a broken pail handle, put the head back on the ax, lock the outhouse door, fix the steps, lash down the henhouse roof, secure the pedal on the spinning wheel, tie the third leg back on the milking stool, keep the shutters from rattling, tighten the hay rack, hang up a lamp, lace your boots, belt up your pants, tie your braids and fix your fiddle—all with binder twine!

But now in the fall of 1926, binder twine has another use to add to the list.

Spinning, wrapping, rolling and tying up a lawyer.

Mean Hughie had him wrapped real tight, apparently.

The lawyer was stiff as a mummy according to the O'Malley girls.

Then Mean Hughie, he put the lawyer on the sawhorse the way you'd throw on a slab of wood, Mayor Even Steven says.

The best way to saw slab wood on a sawhorse is to put one foot up on the middle of the slab to hold it steady while you saw off the end of it. The end that you'd saw off would be right there just about where the lawyer's Adam's Apple was. That's what Great-uncle Ronald supposed.

Mean Hughie had his boot on the lawyer's bellybutton.

And the saw blade on his throat resting nice and easy.

"It'll only hurt quite a bit at first," Mean Hughie explained to the lawyer, "and then soon after that you probably won't feel a thing!" Lucky for the lawyer, Mean Hughie let him go after a while. The lawyer was terrified right out of his wits.

When the lawyer finally got back home in Hull a couple of days later, he told his wife he was quitting being a lawyer and they were never to mention it again. That was that as far as lawyering was concerned!

What was it the lawyer went to tell Mean Hughie that made him so mad? Everybody wants to know. Everybody's buzzing around with the question. What was it the lawyer said?

5

A Surprise Visit

BUT we can't find that out just yet.

Mayor Even Steven is just about to tell us what the lawyer told Mean Hughie when all of a sudden everybody's looking back up the road to where there's a big black, shiny, brand-new car coming right in down and onto the middle of the picnic ground!

"Jesus Mary and Joseph!" says Mayor Even Steven (I never heard him curse before). "He *did* come!"

The car's got a red, white and blue Union Jack flag that looks like a target fluttering on the front. Everybody's running and crowding around and some are clapping and then the doors all open all at once and out comes the driver in a cap and another tall man in a dark blue suit and then the driver has a little platform with a step that he sets up a bit away from the car and runs back and opens the back door of the big shiny car and out comes a short handsome-looking man with a serious square face wearing a tall hard silky top hat and carrying a cane and Mayor Even Steven is falling all over himself trying to get through the crowd and now everybody's clapping and cheering and yes, it is, it's the Prime Minister of Canada, Mr. Mackenzie King, and he's wearing a stiff collar and a tight tie and a vest buttoned up and the shine of his shoes could blind you and with the crease in his pants you could slice a loaf of my mother's bread.

And now Mayor Even Steven is trying to make a speech to tell us all what we already know which is that the Prime Minister of Canada, Prime Minister Mackenzie King, is come to visit us here today and is going to make a short speech because of the election coming but Mayor Even Steven is having an awful time and a lot of trouble saying all this because he's sputtering and stuttering and blushing and backing into people and swallowing and sweating there and everybody's laughing and saying, "Go ahead, Steven, you can do it!" and Prime Minister Mackenzie King is standing there with his cane and hat and tight collar and vest in the September blazing heat looking as cool as a peeled cucumber and our mayor Even Steven is at last done saying whatever he tried to say and everybody gives him a big cheer and the short man steps up the step onto his little platform and the driver in the cap and the tall man in the blue suit stand on either side of him and quiet comes over the crowd until all you can hear is the roar of the Paugan Falls and you can see Mr. Prime Minister Mackenzie King's mouth open and see him start to talk and maybe the ones near the front can hear his little speech but most of us can't but it doesn't matter because everybody enjoys it anyway. Canada is an independent nation after all, whatever that is, but it's good! And everybody cheers their heads off and the lads are jumping back into the water and the driver with the cap puts Mr. Prime Minister Mackenzie King's little platform back in the trunk and opens the door for the Prime Minister and the tall one gets in and the Prime Minister gives a big wave and gets another big cheer and the doors all shut bang bang and the windows roll up and then around and off drives the big slick black car!

Jackie Boyle is standing beside me. He's in my class at school. Jackie's not all there. Even his own mother says so.

"Is he really a king?" says Jackie.

"He sure is, Jackie," I say. "Did you not see his crown?"

"That was a hat, not a crown," says Jackie.

In a while we get Mayor Even Steven calmed down enough to tell us what he was going to tell us before all the fuss started.

"What was it, Steven, that the lawyer said to Mean Hughie that made him so mad?" the O'Malley girls say both at once.

"The lawyer told Mean Hughie that the water was going to come up and cover his farm and that Mean Hughie wouldn't be paid one cent for it because he didn't own it anyway because he didn't have a proper deed for it because he's what is known as a squatter like a lot of other farmers up and down the river!"

Squatters!

Well, Mean Hughie wouldn't like that one bit. It's no wonder they say he tried to remove the lawyer's head from his body with the buck saw!

6
Taking Rocks

WE'RE learning in school about rocks.

When I told my father we were taking rocks in school he said, "Where are you taking them?" Then he laughed and said he was sorry he just couldn't help it and said that it was "a good thing to study rocks because that's what we have most of around here!"

Whenever we work plowing or harrowing or discing our fields in the spring or in the fall kids like us walk behind the machines and pick up rocks, if they're not too heavy, that have been turned up and carry them over and pile them along the fence.

"If we had as many turnips as we had rocks we'd be as rich as J.R. Booth!" my father always likes to say.

There's blue rocks and beige rocks. Bone-colored rocks and rusty red ones. Black rocks with white frozen veins running through. Flat gray hard rocks good for skipping across calm water. Our teacher has a big thick skipper on his desk to hold his papers down. There's rocks the size of houses and the size of peas. And everything in between.

Feldspar and gneiss and quartz and granite are some of the names that will be on the test we're going to have.

These rocks feel cool on your hand. These are the oldest rocks in this world, right here along the Gatineau River.

Up from the center of the earth four billion years ago they came. Massive explosions forced them up here.

"This is boring," says Jackie Boyle.

Then hot lava boiled around until one billion years ago. Liquid rock rolling.

"Why do we have to take rocks again this year?" says Jackie Boyle.

"Most of us weren't in this same class last year, Jackie," I say, trying not to be cruel.

Then these mountains blowing up, shoving up miles into the sky like the Rockies way out west.

"This isn't true," says Jackie Boyle.

Then, hundreds of millions of years ago, water and wind start wearing the mountains away.

"It was God made the rocks, not the water and wind," says Jackie Boyle.

"Your brain reminds me of a rock, Jackie," I say, trying not to be too insulting.

Then, only five hundred million years ago, the sea coming and going, coming and going over top of where we're sitting right now, the earth breathing like a giant in and out, leaving layers and layers and layers...

My head is spinning with the thought of it all.

And then only about a million years ago, the ice age scraping and crushing and pressing the rocks and then fifty thousand years ago melting and moving into rivers and dropping off rocks like seeds.

Seeds from the center of the earth.

Then ten thousand years ago, a great sea forms and whales swim over us.

The great sea then flows out and the rivers and cracks are left and the worn-down old hills.

And then all of a sudden it's now. Rocks and clay and water. I have a feeling of excitement in my stomach.

"This is stupid," says Jackie Boyle.

"Four billion years of hard trying, Jackie Boyle, and all we could come up with was the likes of you," I whisper to Jackie, trying not to hurt his feelings.

After school I tell my friend, Doobie Noonan, that I'm going to kiss Mickey McGuire Jr. one day but I don't know when.

"When? When? When?" says Doobie, all excited. "Tell me when!"

"I don't know when," I say. "But I'm going to."

"Please tell me when you decide—please!"

"I won't know until I know," I tell her.

"If you know when and you have time to tell me, will you tell me?" says Doobie.

"Tell you what? What for?" I say.

"Tell me when you're going to kiss Mickey McGuire Jr. and tell me where. Maybe I can watch!" says Doobie, very excited now.

Suddenly I see somebody hiding behind the schoolyard tree, listening. It's Jackie Boyle.

"Shh!" I say to Doobie. Jackie runs off.

"Did he hear?" says Doobie.

"I hope he didn't," I say. "I hope he didn't."

7
Beauty and Dreams

EVERYBODY says I'm beautiful.

Well, not everybody. My mother never tells me that I'm beautiful. She says it's what's in your heart and in your head that counts and the rest is all nonsense. My father says I'm pretty but that it won't last so don't get depending on it too much like his third cousin Rachel from across the river did and went and spent a lot of her time admiring herself looking into the well till one day she went to kiss herself and fell in and drowned and that was the end of her and her so-called pretty face.

And Jackie Boyle, he didn't say I was beautiful either. He said I looked like an owl because of my big eyes. That was back when I was in grade four when he told me that. Jackie was in grade seven then.

Jackie Boyle is still in grade seven and I'm caught up with him. I suppose you could say, couldn't you, that when you're in your fourth year in the same grade maybe you don't really know a whole lot about what you're talking about?

But they say he might pass this year. On to grade eight, if you please! They should have a parade. Then he'll have to spend four or five years in that grade, I suppose.

Doobie Noonan (she's really good in math) says if Jackie goes right through to the end of high school the way he's going now she figures he'll be over forty years old by the time he gets out. Doobie makes me laugh.

Doobie's older brother, Richard, he's really smart. He's already done high school down in Ottawa and he's going to go to university to study up to be an engineer.

He's going to build dams, he says.

Dams. That's what everybody talks about these days.

Mickey McGuire Jr. explains a dam:

"They put a big wall in the river and pile up the water behind it. Then they put pipes through the wall and let the water roar through them. The force of the water turns big wheels and the turning of the wheels makes electricity. The electricity goes out on wires all over the countryside for electric lights and electric stoves and radios for all the houses and even electric water pumps for the cattle in the barn."

"Won't it be grand we'll all get the electricity first before the others because we're closer to the dam!" I say.

But other people are saying other things.

They're saying that the lawyers of the big company who are building the dam have already promised the electricity to the big cities and have already cut down most of our pine trees to make fancy houses in New York City and we won't even get a lightbulb out of any of it.

And that our fields and houses will be all under water so what does it matter anyway? The water will come up over the top of us, so get ready to swim for it!

Others say it's all a lot of nonsense.

And I'm having these dreams. Poets dream a lot.

I look out my bedroom window at the river way down there across our field, pretty as a picture. The river slipping by there pretty quick but without a sound, it's so deep and slick and smooth.

Not like a couple of valleys away, down at the falls, where we have the picnics where they'll put the dam where the same water is boiling and roaring and rearing up madder than a beaten horse, wild and frothing at the mouth.

In my dreams the river outside my bedroom window, slippy and silent as a snake, is coming coiling up across the field and sliding and sidling slow up and lifting and floating away our henhouse, sneaky and pretty as you please and cuter than the fox or the weasel, then licking up to our doorstep and then coming in the door onto the kitchen floor—oh, look what's come for an unexpected visit, what a surprise—and then I wake up in a terror and call out and my mother sometimes comes into my room with the lamp flickering and whispers never mind to me and tucks me in and I feel like such a baby and ride back to sleep while I think I'm far too old and big to be tucked in by me ma and whispered to but I'm glad she does it anyway and goodnight river.

Doobie Noonan (her real name's Deborah) says she never dreams. Says dreaming's a waste of time. When you go to sleep, that's the time for sleeping, she says, not dreaming. The time for dreaming, she says, is when you're awake, in the daytime. And she has some daydreams that she tells me about that I would never repeat here to you.

Sometimes they're about Andy Ryan, the heartthrob of the municipality of Low. Andy Ryan is quite a bit older than Doobie Noonan.

She goes in on purpose and tells these dreams to Father Foley in her confession but she never mentions Andy Ryan by name. Making up a lot of it as she goes along, she says. That's what daydreaming is, she says. It's stuff you make up when your mind has nothing to do.

We were talking about beauty.

Father Foley doesn't say I'm beautiful. He says beauty is in the eye of the beholder. I almost know what that means and I'm waiting for the rest of it to come to me. I think, though, it's something to do with Mrs. McSorely. Mrs. McSorely brings her baby into McLaughlan's store just about every day. She keeps saying to everybody around, "Isn't he beautiful?" while everybody pretty well knows that little Ambrose McSorely is probably the ugliest baby on the face of the earth (he has a head like a big crooked potato) but nobody will make Mrs. McSorely feel bad by saying it in front of her.

Doobie doesn't call me beautiful. Doobie calls me curly. Not because my hair is curly. My hair is reddish brown and wavy but it's not what you call curly.

It's my face that's curly. My eyes are curly, my cheeks are curly, my lips are curly, my eyelashes are curly, my nose is curly. My whole face is all curves and curls.

So those that say I'm beautiful say that it's in a curly sort of way.

The main person who doesn't say I'm beautiful is me. I look in the mirror. I think I'm too curly.

And anyway, it doesn't matter. It's what's in your heart and in your head that counts and the rest is all nonsense.

That's what I always say.

8

Dolomitic

AT our farm the river is wide and quiet and smooth and doesn't look like it's moving, but it is. If you get out there in your boat you don't have to row very much at all to float down the river to the falls.

As you float, soon the water gets faster and the river gets rougher and narrower and the shores get higher and higher and things get louder.

Soon you'll find yourself in a narrow hallway with straight high rock walls. Our teacher, Patchy Drizzle, says the walls are made of crystalline limestone, probably dolomitic, he says. Because it's limestone the rushing water for millions of years has made shapes and caves and tunnels along the cliffs. Marble statues of shapes from another world.

The water pouring past and in and out of these caves and shapes makes so many different sounds that it's hard to think straight.

Patchy Drizzle says it's like a massive symphony orchestra all playing a different song with no leader or anybody to keep it all from going haywire.

You keep to the right wall where the water's not so fast. You hold the boat with the oars.

Soon you are looking at something that's hard to believe until you get used to it. The river looks like it stops. You're floating right into a rock wall. It's not a wall as high as the walls on the sides are but it's high enough. About as high as our farmhouse.

Stay on your right and go to the corner and steer your boat into a small cave there where you're safe. The water helps you here because it's pushing backwards up to where you came from.

The water goes to the wall, turns left for about twenty lengths of the boat then tears to the right through a narrow gorge and roars over and disappears. That's our Paugan Falls.

It pours over a cliff about as high as the cross is on the top of the steeple over Mary Ann Alice the bell of St. Martin's Church. But you'll never hear the bell from here for the roar.

The roar of the water tearing over a cliff made of granite that'll never wear out.

Our teacher, Patchy Drizzle, is on the skinny side and tall but he has wide shoulders. His hair is sandy colored and his eyes are blue. He has a kind mouth, fair skin and sticky-out ears.

When Patchy Drizzle talks about dolomitic and granite and other kinds of rocks and mountains and millions of years and flowing water his face gets a happy look, his eyes get bright and excited. And he stands up straight and tall.

When he goes to teach he always puts on a special hat. It's a bowler hat. A black round hat with a brim that you see pictures of fancy gentlemen wearing in Eaton's catalogue, if you please. It's hard and silky like Prime Minister Mackenzie King's hat only it's short and round, not square and tall.

In the holidays when the weather is lovely and bright, Patchy Drizzle aches to go down the gorge in his boat and crawl around those caves playing with the rocks there, touching them, collecting them, rubbing them, studying the walls, the shapes. He says there's messages there from a billion years ago.

His boat has the name *The Dolomite* printed on the bow.

Patchy lives with his wife in a little white house with flowers in pots in the windows just up the hill from the school.

Patchy used to take his wagon and load his rowboat on and haul it up to our farm and put it in the river at our dock and float down to the caves that way. Now he leaves the boat at our place. Saves bringing it back and forward all the time. And he's going more and more to the caves. Even in bad weather. He's at home less and less.

Even at night. With a lantern and a battery light.

Jackie Boyle says Patchy Drizzle, the best teacher in the world, is crazy.

"Did you see the name he has wrote on his boat? The Dynamite? What kind of a name of a boat is that? Dynamite?" says Jackie.

"It's Dolomite, Jackie," I say. "It's a kind of rock formation that has hollow spaces in it. A lot like your head," I say to Jackie, trying my very best to be as kind as I possibly can to him.

When Patchy's finished teaching and the kids leave the schoolhouse, he takes off his bowler hat and puts it on the top shelf inside his cupboard and shuts the door very gentle like he's just put a baby to bed and then goes out and up the hill to his house with the geraniums in the windows.

The closer to home he gets, the more stooped over he gets, looking down at his feet moving out in front of him.

Like his feet aren't his own or something.

Today we have a rock test. The seven of us in grade seven. The others, the sixes and fives, and the little ones in grade one to four are doing other work—coloring, pasting, reading, writing.

Patchy has placed rocks along the long table at the side of the room. Each rock has a little tag attached with a question written on. You go along the table with your pad and you answer the questions the rocks ask you. And you keep your pad close to your chest so the others won't look over your shoulder.

"This is the same as last year," says Jackie Boyle. Jackie's right behind me. He's looking over my shoulder.

There's twenty-five rocks asking twenty-five questions.

What am I? What mineral is in me? What is my name? How old am I? What brought me here? Am I alive? What will happen to me? When was I on fire? When did I fly miles into the sky? How long was I under water? Under ice? Am I buried treasure? Am I a semi-precious stone? Why do they call me fool's gold?

Questions like that.

I make two sets of answers. The right answers and another list of wrong answers I make up as I go along. The second list I keep away from my chest. I hold it out a bit so's Jackie Boyle can see it and copy it down. He's so close behind me I can feel his breath on my ear. Go ahead, Jackie.

Just trying to help. So I look like an owl, do I?

After, when everybody's gone, I stay back and help Patchy take the tags off the rocks and put each rock back in its place on the shelves and in the glass cupboards on their little cushions.

"When they flood the river," says Patchy, "those caves will be buried under water so deep that nobody will ever see them again. All the treasure there will be hidden from us for lifetimes, spoiled probably forever."

Treasure. Patchy is standing tall.

Outside at the window I see Jackie Boyle's head disappear.

Patchy puts his bowler hat careful in the high cupboard, shuts the door silent so's not to wake up the hat that's like a baby and goes out.

I watch him go up the hill to his house.

Head down, watching his feet go out in front of him. Going somewhere where he doesn't want to go.

Jackie Boyle's alongside of me.

"Buried treasure, is it?" says Jackie.

The look on him tells me that he thinks he's finally, at last, got something right.

"And I know something else," says Jackie. "I know yer gonna kiss Mickey McGuire Jr. and Doobie Noonan's going to watch!"

"You better not tell anybody that, Jackie!"

"Maybe I will, maybe I won't," says Jackie.

"You do, and I'll rip your tongue out!" I say.

9

The Corks

I'LL go up the river today to have a little visit with the Corks. Mickey McGuire Jr. says he desperately wants to come along with me because he hasn't seen the Corks for quite a while and he can hardly stand it never seeing them for so long and he misses them so much.

But I know that's not quite true. It's not that he wants to visit the Corks so much. It's more likely that he wants to try and kiss me behind the shed just like the other time we went up there and I wouldn't let him.

That's all right. He can row the boat up. I'll row back. It's three quarters of an hour hard pull up there. Over one rapids and around another one. Easy to come back though.

I like Mickey McGuire Jr. Maybe it's because I know what he's thinking all the time. And he's a good rower. I like to watch his strong hands on the oars.

The Cork farm is on the other side of the river and way up. The lonesome side. There's no roads over there. There's no other farms close to the Corks. They're all alone.

Their farm is right on the river shore in a lovely meadow but back behind it is a high cliff. They have two fields. They have a house of two floors. The main part of the house is logs. The top part is boards. The roof is tin. They have a barn, a stable, a woodshed, a chicken coop, a pig pen, a milk shack and a root cellar. All made of logs. And a shed. And the outhouse which is a four-holer. My father says it's the only *four*-holer in the whole countryside.

"For a family of five it's the very best," my father says. "Grampa, the son, the son's wife and the youngest kid can all go to the little house and sit there in a row together. The oldest kid stays in the house to tend the stove. Specially in the winter you can keep warm together while you're sitting close like that and maybe smoke a pipe and have a family discussion with the lamp flickering away there, ah, it must be just grand altogether!"

The Corks have a horse, some cows, a few pigs, a dog, many cats and a rooster.

Grampa Cork is lying sick in a bed downstairs in the kitchen. He coughs all the time and every now and then he leans out of the bed and spits a big yellow and green one into an old pail. A cat runs over and looks in.

Mr. and Mrs. Cork both look the same. They both smoke clay pipes and they have the same kind of hair and the same nose like a round button.

Their two kids—the girl Rowan, the lad Balder—are together all the time. Now and then they come to school but not very often. They never say much of anything.

Patchy says Rowan is named after the rowan tree which has magic red berries and Balder is the name of the good and beautiful myth god of the Vikings. The god Balder had a dream that he would be killed so all the other gods had a big meeting and got promises from everything that could ever hurt or kill you like fire or water or rocks or trees or disease or animals and everything so's Balder would always be safe and never in any danger. But one bad god, a jealous one, went and found out that they left out one thing that could kill you, which was, believe it or not, mistletoe. So Balder was killed by mistletoe.

Mickey McGuire Jr. is hauling away with all his might on the oars and we're moving on pretty good. I'm telling all about what Patchy told us about the myth god of the Vikings and the mistletoe.

The sun is almost over the top of us and the Gatineau River water is gurgling by the boat. I know exactly what Mickey is going to say.

"Mistletoe's fer kissin' under I always thought," says Mickey. "Ya hang it over the door and—"

"Keep rowing the boat, Mickey McGuire Jr. You're doin' just fine!" I say. This is neither the time nor the place, Mickey, I say to myself.

Then Mickey says something I don't expect him to say. Something that surprises me.

"You're always hanging around after school talkin' to Patchy. Are ya in love with him or something?" says Mickey.

"Don't be ridiculous, Mickey," I say.

Can you believe it? Mickey is jealous. Jealous of me and Patchy Drizzle! A man old enough to be my father!

We cut up through the Last Little Rapids and pull up along the Cork wharf.

Their rowboat is tied there, half full of water. Their rowboat leaks.

When the Corks row down to our farm once a week or so to get a ride to Low for supplies or to bring a can or two of sour cream to sell to the butter and cheese factory, you can hear them on the river long before you see them round the point into the bay.

What you hear is two sounds.

One sound is of one of the oars squeaking in the oarlock. One, two, three, squeak! One, two, three, squeak!

The other sound is the bailing can scraping the bottom of the boat, bailing out the water.

One Cork rows, the other Cork has to bail.

If one Cork doesn't keep bailing, the boat will fill with water and sink.

Now and then Patchy will turn their boat over for them at our shore and stuff the seams with horse hair and patch in some hot tar but the boat always goes back to leaking anyway.

We pick our way through the first field along the winding clay path. The path curves out near the edge of the field along the rock fence. One part of the rock fence is built high and there's a cross.

A grave. Grampa Cork's mother and father.

Peter Cork

b. Ireland 1827   d. Here Dec 21, 1900

Constance Cork

b. Ireland 1830   d. Here Dec 21, 1900

In the house Grampa Cork waves to us from the bed like a man going away on a long trip.

He's praying out loud and going over his beads. The only time he stops praying is when he coughs and then leans out of the bed to spit in the pail.

There's two cats asleep on the bed.

Mrs. Cork fusses over us like a mother partridge, telling me how beautiful I am and Mickey how handsome he is.

Mickey believes her but I don't.

Mrs. Cork cuts slices of hot bread just out of the oven and makes us tomato sandwiches with salt and pepper. The tomatoes are hot, too, because I just picked them off the vine in the yard, right out there in the open in the warm sun.

The sweet butter drips out of the sandwich down my wrist. There's a chicken under the kitchen table. And three cats.

Mickey goes out to look for Mr. Cork and I go up the steep narrow stairs to see the kids. Some cats follow me up.

I stop on the stairs when the second floor is about to my waist and lean on my elbows there.

Balder and Rowan are playing silent up here. The floor is covered with their toys. Curls of wood shavings, the dried corpses of bugs, slices of mica, smooth rolled little stones from the center of the earth, white fishhead skeletons, twisted knuckle bony roots, sticky gum pine cones, wizened gooseberries, a stiff pig's tail with the curl and a little framed picture of Lord Jesus himself with the thorns around his head and the drops of blood coming down into his eyes.

There's at least one cat in each corner.

There's oak leaves and dried mistletoe around the window. The mistletoe is very old and has a gold color.

Back downstairs, Grampa Cork spits in his pail. Two cats run over and look in.

Outside, Mr. Cork's telling Mickey and me about the lawyers.

"There was two of them. And a third and a fourth lad to row the boat. Big boat. Two sets of oars. I didn't see it. Only Grampa was here. We were all away hunting. Last fall. Grampa signed the papers. The lawyers told him what was on the papers. Grampa can't read too well. Specially that kind of writing. Who can read that kind of writing, only lawyers? They said that the water will come up and cover part of our field. And that we'd be paid for it as soon as it was up to where it was going to come up to. Something like that. Grampa said they had the finest leather briefcases he's ever felt. Even in New York City when he was there once. But you know something, I hate to say this but I don't think Grampa's ever been to New York City but you never know!" Mr. Cork looks off in the distance towards the river. Then he looks back at us. "I'd love to take a peek into one of them fancy briefcases of theirs," says Mr. Cork.

Mickey and I take a long walk in up around the back

and get right up on the high cliff behind the Cork farm.

You can see many things from up here.

This cliff is straight down. Like pictures you see of the big ocean liner ships they're building before they slide them into the sea. We're on the ship right at the front.

Corks' little toy farm is way, way straight down there.

You can see Dizzy Peak from here (there's no ark on it) and Mary Ann Alice's steeple over there at Martindale and the village of Low. And is that mist way down there from the Paugan Falls and the little clouds and the circling birds and the blue sky and all the trees and all the rocks...Oh, my! I'm aching with the beauty of it all.

Oh, how I wish they'd ring Mary Ann Alice right now.

I'd love to hear the bell now, clear and pretty across the valley!

"There's that shed down there," says Mickey McGuire Jr. "Where we were the last time we were here." I can see through Mickey like a window.

Not yet, Mickey.

"So it is," I say, and I take off back down the side of the mountain into the trees, him chasing me. And down across the field and onto the wharf and into the boat and row away.

We get back down the river to my farm and my wharf and tie up.

It's just about dark. The moon's peekin'.

Patchy Drizzle's boat was there when we left today at noon.

But it's not there now.

10

Miserable Mrs. Drizzle

IN McLaughlan's store I'm picking over some new gum boots with the special rough treads on the bottoms so's I won't slip when I go crawling around the cliffs and the caves to find rocks for my collection.

The best set of boots costs $1.90.

In comes Mrs. McSorely with her baby, Ambrose.

"Isn't he beautiful?" says Mrs. McSorely to Mr. McLaughlan behind the counter. He's in his big brown apron. The store smells lovely of spices and leather boots and licorice.

"He's a pure delight!" says Mr. McLaughlan to Mrs. McSorely. He's lying but it's all right.

My mother always says never lie unless you have to so's to save somebody's feelings. And never lie to damage anybody's feelings. And don't forget: What they don't know won't hurt them!

Little baby Ambrose is looking extra ugly today. The other day he looked like a big crooked potato. Today it's hard to say what he looks like. Something that's just been boiled, maybe.

Into the store comes Mrs. Victoria Drizzle, Patchy Drizzle's wife. She's a tall woman with a long face and large teeth. She's dressed nice and neat.

Mrs. Drizzle is from England. She has a snooty kind of accent on her. Instead of saying potato like a normal human being she says put-*taw*-tow. Make your lips in a circle.

Doobie Noonan is really good at languages. She's good at pronouncing. She says that when Mrs. Drizzle hears *us* say the word potato, she actually hears the word pid-*day*-dah. Open your mouth wide. PID-*DAY*-DAH!

Mrs. McSorely turns to Mrs. Drizzle, showing the baby.

"Good morning, Mrs. Drizzle. Is it a lovely morning or what? I've got little Ambrose along with me to help me shop. You're helping me, aren't you, darlin'? Isn't he beautiful, Mrs. Drizzle?"

Mrs. Victoria Drizzle looks at Ambrose.

Her small mouth gets smaller and her upper lip curls a bit and her nose wrinkles up like something rotten just fell down the chimney.

"On the contrary, Mrs. McSorely. Your baby, as a matter of fact, is extraordinarily ugly. One could almost say it hardly looks like a baby at all!"

Poor Mrs. McSorely. She should have known better. Mr. McLaughlan knew what was coming. I knew what was coming. Everybody in town would have known better 'n to ask Mrs. Drizzle for a little consideration.

My father once said that Father Foley told him in all confidence that Mrs. Drizzle had a mouth on her like the south end of a hen.

Now, that's just not true.

My father often says that Father Foley says things that, of course, he never said. A priest would never say a thing like that about a person in the parish. Well, actually Mrs. Drizzle is not one of us, she's a Protestant, so she's not really in our parish as far as St. Martin's Church is concerned but still, Father Foley wouldn't even say that about a Protestant.

Not even a Protestant the likes of Mrs. Drizzle.

My mother told me all about Mrs. Drizzle. Patchy was overseas in the war and then in England in the hospital there and she was a nurse and when he got better (a bomb blew him up in the air), he came back home to Low and had her with him. Already married.

"War makes you do foolish things," my mother said. "Bringing her away over here was the wrong thing to do. She hates it here, she hates Low, she hates the Gatineau, she hates us all here, she hates her husband Patchy. We knew as soon as we laid eyes on her and heard her and met her that she didn't fit and that her and poor Patchy didn't fit and now they're stuck together forever I suppose. Big mistake."

Now the baby's howling and Mrs. McSorely takes him out. Her face is red with hurt.

Mrs. Drizzle is sipping air through her little mouth. That's the way she breathes. She sips, like she's breathing through a straw.

My father says that Father Foley told him in all confidence that she breathes like that so's she won't suck in any of the big lumps of manure that she thinks are flying around the country like tennis balls.

Nothing Mr. McLaughlan has in his store is right for Mrs. Drizzle. He's weighed the sugar wrong. He's weighed the flour wrong. He's tied the pound bag of beans too tight. The molasses jar is sticky. The coal oil can isn't full to the top. The fly stickers aren't the right brand. She wants Tanglefoot not Trapstick. The eggs aren't brown enough. There's a bubble in one of the mason jars. The tea's not English tea.

Mrs. Drizzle is sipping air through her little mouth. "Have you ever been to England, Mr. McLaughlan?" she says. Sip. Sip.

"Can't say that I have," says Mr. McLaughlan. "Had a cousin went to Ottawa, though. Drove a milk delivery there. Then drove a bread wagon. Switched to delivering ice. Then coal. Then slab wood, house to house. Coal was the worst. Coal and ice. And wood. Milk was heavy but not as dirty as coal or wood or ice. Bread is what he liked the best. Bread was a good one to deliver. Light to carry. Smelled good. Everybody was glad to see you comin'. Everything pleasant, nobody mad or sour or anything like that..." Poor Mr. McLaughlan, tryin' his best.

"If you went to England, Mr. McLaughlan, you would discover that the shops there carry the very best brands of produce and never any shoddy ware!" Sip. Sip.

"Another cousin o' mine, Hulbert Dile, went to

Chicago once just to look around. Never come back," says Mr. McLaughlan.

"I'm not surprised," says Mrs. Drizzle. "Why would anyone want to come back to this dreadful place?" Time to go.

The little bell on the top of the door jingles and now she's gone.

I ask Mr. McLaughlan would he put aside the gum boots for me and my father would come in and pay for them. He tells me to go ahead and take them and he'll settle up with my father next time he sees him.

Mr. McLaughlan never says anything bad about anybody. I'm looking into his big kind face. We're reading each other's minds, not saying a word. Mr. McLaughlan shakes his head once and presses his lips together.

Is that the most miserable, the sourest, most hateful individual you've ever met in all o' yer born days? says Mr. McLaughlan's face without even one word coming out of him.

I'm just about to say something even better than that about Mrs. Victoria Drizzle but I can't. I can't because the floor of Mr. McLaughlan's store is trembling. The cups and saucers and glass lamp chimneys on his shelves are tinkling. And there's a rumbling.

"They're blasting," says Mr. McLaughlan. "They're starting the dam! It's the beginning of the end!"

11

Rocks in the Box

THEY'VE built a city here!

In two months they built a city!

From Martindale Road all the way down to the falls, right over our picnic ground, there's a city. With dozens of buildings and roadways and intersections. There's hundreds and hundreds of men from around here and from everywhere else working on the dam. For the first time nobody's hunting deer this fall. Usually everything shuts down and most of the men go out hunting. They even shut the school. This year, though, everything is shut but nobody's hunting. Everybody's working at the dam site. Even the older kids from school.

I'm working here. I'm a waitress. I wait on tables. I feed the men in mess hall number one. There's twelve mess halls. There's one hundred lads eat in my mess hall.

I make fifteen cents an hour.

There's two breakfasts, two dinners, two suppers. Fifty of the lads eat their breakfast at six o'clock in the morning in my mess hall number one. Then another fifty pile in at half past six for theirs. That's a hundred breakfasts.

Then they come back, the first fifty, half starved, at twelve noon and gobble up their dinner. And they'd better not eat slow because the second fifty are right in on top of them at twelve-thirty and they're even hungrier.

Then at six o'clock in the evening the first fifty are back for their supper and some of them are so hungry they're frothin' at the mouth and then they're no sooner done than the second fifty are banging on the door threatening to chew their own legs off if you don't let them in and feed them!

Remember Mrs. Kealey? She makes the stew for the church picnics. Now she's in charge of our cookhouse. The cookhouse is attached to the mess hall in the middle at the back. There's two big wood stoves in there and four big sinks with running water for doin' dishes and cleaning. There's four women doin' dishes and cleaning. There's one lad who all he does is keep the fires going. There's me and two or three other girls who do the serving.

Patchy told me that my job was one of the most important jobs on the whole dam site. He said that even though there's plenty of engines run by gas and electricity and steam and even though there's horses to do heavy work, too, the most important machines on the job are the human machines. And human machines need fuel or they won't be able to work.

Food is fuel. I bring the fuel to the human machines who are building the dam. Pretty important.

But sometimes I wonder, if it's so important, why am I making fifteen cents an hour and every one of the machines I bring the fuel to are making twenty cents an hour?

The other day some of the lads in the first load of fifty started chanting my name to make the food-fuel come faster.

"Mary Ann Alice! Mary Ann Alice!"

And while they chanted they banged on the table with a fork in one fist and a knife in the other fist.

Now they're all doing it. And it's making my face red and I'm afraid I'm going to drop some plates full of meat-loaf or bowls of boiled potatoes. Or one of the big milk jugs full of gravy.

"Mary Ann Alice! Mary Ann Alice!" goes the chant.

Now here comes Mrs. Kealey from the cookhouse into the mess hall. She has with her her big long-handled wood-en spoon. She brings down the flat of the spoon hard on the top of the long center table. The whack is like a rifle shot.

Everybody shuts up. Everything stops.

"Gentlemen!" she says, not yelling but good and strong and loud. "Gentlemen, there'll be no more chanting names or banging on the tables. The next person with any notions about acting rude with any of my hard-working girls here does not get served a plate. Do you hear me, lads? You don't get anything to eat! And if you don't believe me, why don't you just give it a try!"

There's a bit of mumbling but that's definitely the end of that. There'll be no more chanting.

These lads would sooner have their heads chopped off than go without their dinner.

It's hard to believe how much they eat. Mrs. Kealey showed me the other day a list of the supplies she got shipped in to her for twenty-one days of eating. I kept the list to show to Patchy Drizzle. I wrote this at the top of the page:

Fuel List for Building Dam.

Five cows
Twenty pigs
One hundred chickens
Three hundred fish
Four hundred bowls of butter
Six hundred dozen eggs
Nine hundred pails of milk
Six hundred bags of potatoes
One hundred bags of flour
Twelve hundred shovelfuls of beans
Two thousand bags of sugar
Six hundred cans of tea and coffee
Eight thousand cans of canned goods
A cartload of onions
One barrel of lard

And that's just the fuel for the human machines in mess hall number one!

My hundred lads are workin' on what they call the By-Pass. The By-Pass is a long deep tunnel through the granite. They're going to make the whole river run through there while they're building the dam at the falls.

Patchy explained it to us.

They drill down into the granite, then they dynamite the rock and it falls in big pieces.

Then my hundred hungry lads break it up with sledges, pick the pieces up with their bare hands and lift the pieces into big boxes. They call themselves the Rocks in the Box Gang.

Then the boxes get hoisted and dumped into railway cars right there where they built a special railway track. The train hauls away the rocks to the crusher.

Besides the mess halls there's bunkhouses and bath houses. Each bunkhouse has sixty metal bedsteads, mattresses and blankets and a big stove in the center. The bath houses have hot and cold running water, sinks, showers, electric lights and toilets.

My father says the bath houses are just like the ones they have at the fanciest hotel in the world, the Waldorf Astoria in New York City, except for the horrible smell.

There's also other buildings—houses for families, offices, engineers' quarters, stores, barber shops and a hospital building for cuts and bruises and broken bones. And there's even a little police station where Mean Bone McCooey and two young ruffians go round at night to make sure everybody's behaving.

Everybody's working here.

The O'Malley girls are working in the little two-room hospital patching up the wounded with their special recipes and remedies. Mayor Even Steven is some kind of a supervisor. Great-uncle Ronald is on the night watch.

Mean Hughie is on the rock crusher. Most of the McCooeys are back and forward delivering this and that. Patchy is on part-time duty helping the big chief engineer himself with the geology of the rocks. Mr. McLaughlan is helping the man in charge of all the tools. Doobie Noonan is in the barber shop sweeping up hair and sometimes even getting to cut a head or two.

She's watching out the window. Maybe Andy Ryan needs to come in to get his hair cut. You never know.

And I'm glad to say that all this has made her completely forget what I told her about me and Mickey McGuire Jr.

And even Jackie Boyle is working! He is, after all, seventeen years of age. He's a helper with the crew working on the power. The electricity they brought up from the new dam at Chelsea. He's pretty puffed up and full up with himself, making twenty cents an hour, if you please. Jackie Boyle making twenty cents an hour.

And me only making fifteen cents.

They don't, I guess, pay you for brains around here.

Or beauty.

"I hear tell y'er only makin' fifteen cents an hour, Mary Ann Alice," he says. "And, in case you don't know, I'm makin' twenty cents an hour!"

"That'd be about five cents more than I'm making an hour, Jackie. Would that be right?"

"I guess," he says.

I almost say, "Don't try to figure it out too fast, Jackie. You might hurt yourself!"but I don't. I figure if I'm a bit nicer to Jackie, he'll forget about blabbing about me and you know who.

Yes, pretty near everybody around is working at what they call the Dam Site except possibly one individual. Mrs. Patchy Drizzle.

12

Wakefield to Drizzle

I KNOCK on the door of Patchy's neat little house up the hill behind the school. It's snowing a bit and Thanksgiving is coming up and hunting season will be over and school will be soon open again and I haven't seen Patchy for a while and I have to ask him about a few beautifully colored rocks one of my hundred lads brought in for me from dynamiting the By-Pass.

A geranium plant in the window moves with a hand on the curtain. Then Mrs. Victoria Drizzle opens the door.

"May I help you?" Mrs. Drizzle's got on her coat and hat. She must be either just comin' in or she's heading out somewhere.

"I'm sorry to bother you, Mrs. Drizzle, but is Mr. Drizzle here?"

"Are you one of Mr. Drizzle's students?"

"Yes, ma'am."

"What is your name, child? Didn't I see you in McLaughlan's shop?"

"Mary Ann Alice McCrank, ma'am." I'm not a child, I'll have you know.

"Mary Ann Alice McCrank. Well, Mary Ann Alice *McCrank*, Mr. Drizzle is not here right now and I'm presently going out on several errands so you'll have to excuse me." Sip.

She shuts the door. I hear her say "McCrank" behind the door. I go down the road a piece and look back and see Mrs. Drizzle leave the house and head up the hill toward the post office.

A minute later there's Patchy comin' up the hill toward me carrying his geology bag he always has with him.

I'm carrying a bag, too. A cloth bag with a few rocks in.

"Mary Ann Alice, you've got rocks there I can tell."

"I do."

"Were you looking for me?"

"I was."

"Did you go to my place?"

"I did."

"Is there anyone there?"

"Not now."

"Come on back up, then."

We go back up and in.

Patchy takes off his coat and puts a big stick in the stove and opens the draft to make the fire roar a bit.

We sit at the table and he spreads out a cloth and takes out his bag and I spread out my rocks and he has his little hammer and his magnifying glass and his little glass bottles of chemicals and his emery paper and buffer cloth.

My rocks. A beautiful smooth round pink hard stone. Granite. Igneous. Igneous means born in fire millions of years ago.

A chunk of limestone. Add a billion years of heat and pressure, you get marble.

A slab of mica. Thin, layered, flexible, transparent, resistant to heat and electricity.

Feeling the mica reminds me of the other day in Patchy's class when we took mica and how it resists electricity. Jackie Boyle got all worked up over it at our desk.

"That's not true," said Jackie. "Electricity can go troo anything. Even rocks."

"You're an expert now in electricity, are ya, Jackie!" I said.

"That's right," he said. "I am."

"What'd y' do, get a shock one time?" I said, making my voice sweet.

"Maybe," said Jackie.

"Well, why don't you give the rest of the world a shock as well and get passed out of grade seven for a change!" I said, trying to be as pleasant as I could to him.

Mrs. Drizzle is back. She hangs up her coat and comes and stands over the table watching us. Patchy stops talking. He acts different when she's there.

"McCrank," says Mrs. Drizzle. "What an odd name. In England a crank is an individual given over to strange ideas and eccentric behavior. And Mc or Mac means son of. So I take it that your father, presumably a Mr. McCrank, is the son of a very odd and queer person."

She's sipping away. She's enjoying herself making fun of my name.

"Of course, a crank is also a handle for turning a wheel. Perhaps your father is the son of a handle! How very entertaining, don't you think, Peter?" (Patchy's real name is Peter.)

"Did you know, Victoria," says Patchy, "that Mary Ann Alice is named after the bell in the steeple of her church, St. Martin's in Martindale?"

"Oh, really! A handle and now a bell! What delightfully quaint customs!" Sip.

My head's starting to get hot. When my head starts to get hot I know that I'm starting to get mad. And when I get mad I sometimes say things I shouldn't say.

Mrs. Drizzle's not done yet.

"Do you know what my name was before I married Mr. Drizzle here?"

"No, ma'am, I don't," I say. My head is on fire.

"My name was Wakefield. An ancient and honorable English name. Miss Victoria Wakefield. I traded, changed my name from Wakefield to Drizzle! Quite a comedown that was, don't you think, Mary Ann Alice McCrank? Wakefield to Drizzle!"

Out of my mouth comes this:

"Wake Field. Does your name Wakefield mean your mother and father woke up in a field one morning and then you were born? Like a cow or a pig?" My mouth. Sometimes it goes to work and says things that I don't even tell it to!

13

A Little Present

I'M telling my mother about getting pushed out of Mrs. Drizzle's because of what I said to her about her name, Wakefield.

About how she was sipping air so quick I thought she was going to choke and about how she threw my coat at me while I was gathering up my rocks from off the cloth on the table. And about how poor Patchy was trying to help me on with my coat and stuff the rocks into my bag at the same time and how my hat was on crooked on my head and how when I glanced quick into the hall mirror while she was rushing me through the door I saw my face as curly as I've ever seen it.

And about how then, on the little front verandah, Patchy stood out there in the blowing snow with me telling me not to worry and then he says wait a minute and he goes in and comes back out and slips me his little geology hammer into my bag and says he'll see me later. A little present. And about how strange and afraid I felt when I walked down the road.

My mother tells me that the reason I felt so strange and afraid as I walked down the road was that nobody's ever been mad at me before and that feeling somebody's anger at me was a brand-new experience for me, for sure! Then she says this:

"Now I'm not saying that what you did was wrong, Mary Ann Alice. Mrs. Drizzle can be very rude at times. I've heard her. And there's no excuse for her carrying on that way with a guest in her own house. I've talked to Mrs. Drizzle a few times, just the two of us, and she can be very pleasant if she puts her mind to it. But she doesn't very often want to put her mind to it." My mother's making a speech. When she decides to speechify there's no stopping her.

"What's wrong with her, anyway?" I say to my mother even though I know she's going to tell me if I ask or if I don't.

"She's a long, long way from home, Mrs. Drizzle is, Victoria Wakefield is. She has no loved ones here, she has no relatives, no friends, she has nothing around that's familiar, she hears nothing she likes, the accent, the words, the lilt of what she hears, the faith we all follow, the four seasons, the water the rocks and trees, the hills and the sky, the sounds, the ways we have, the food, the manners, the things we care about, the things we laugh at and cry about. Everything, everything is strange to her. And the worst of it. When she got here with Patchy, she found out, too late, that she doesn't like him either!"

It's quite a speech.

"Imagine, Mary Ann Alice, yourself, being stuck in a completely strange and foreign place with somebody you don't like and who doesn't like you! Wouldn't that be the most terrible thing?"

"I guess it would," I say and I get to thinking about it. How lonely it would be.

Now, I hope I don't but I think I might start to cry.

My father comes in from the kitchen.

He's putting on his hat and coat.

"I heard the tail end of what you were saying," he says. "You know something, I was only just talking to Father Foley the other day on the very subject of Mrs. Victoria Drizzle and poor Patchy. And Father Foley told me in all confidence that back in the old country, in England, Mrs. Drizzle was a dancer and an acrobat and a trapeze artist in a traveling circus! Can you believe it?"

My father goes out and slams the door.

"No, we don't believe it, Frank! Not a word of it!" my mother calls behind him.

All of a sudden I'm laughing whether I want to or not. I can see Mrs. Drizzle the way she is dressed and the way she talks, doing handsprings and swinging away up there on a trapeze in her little tight costume. Sip. Sip!

I love my father. He can change a tear to a laugh in a heartbeat!

14

Dam Site

TWO dreams.

One, we're in school with Patchy. It's a blowing cold winter day but the stove's cozy and warm and I'm proud of the way it's behaving because it's my week in charge of lighting the fire and keeping it going each day. I always have the best dry kindling and the perfect-sized sticks of maple and birch to keep it glowing the whole day.

My father always prepares the cleanest, driest kindling and hardwood for me to take when it's my week. "That way," he says, "you'll always have the respect of the others." And he's right because whenever it's my turn, I hear the others say, "Good, it's Mary Ann Alice's week so we'll be fine! We'll be cozy and warm!"

Patchy's teaching us something about the way wild rivers, like animals, get mad when you try to tame them with dams but he's getting irritated because Jackie Boyle won't shut up.

"Jackie," says Patchy in my dream, "do you think you

could go ten whole minutes keeping your mouth shut, not saying a word?"

"Why do you say that?" says Jackie. Jackie, in my dream, looks like a grown man about fifty years old. He has a beard on him turning white.

"Because," says Patchy, "I have a proposition for you. If you can shut up for ten whole minutes, I'll pay you two cents for each minute. Two cents a minute for ten minutes. How much would that be, Jackie, if you can do it?"

There's silence.

"Never mind," says Patchy. "When the clock there reaches ten minutes to twelve, we'll start to count. When the clock strikes twelve, the last chime of twelve, and you haven't opened your mouth and said one word, I'll hand you over twenty cents. Here it is right here on the desk!"

He'll do it, says Jackie.

The wind's grabbing at the windows and the pendulum of the clock is tick-tocking away the minutes. Five to twelve. One to twelve. Twelve o'clock! The chimes begin to strike. One. Two. Three. Nine to go.

"I'm goin' to do it!" cries Jackie. "I'm goin' to make it!"

Everybody's laughing and ripping around saying how stupid he is and Jackie gets up and he's awful big and fearsome angry and he kicks over the stove and walks right through the wall of the school out into the storm and there's fire and screaming everywhere...

The other dream is Patchy. He gets out of his boat and goes into one of the caves with his geology bag.

In the cave there's another cave. He ducks in there.

Patchy lights a torch. He's also got a battery light. The walls of the cave he feels. He feels the millions of years there. The markings made by the years and years of time. The chimes of time. The school clock is striking.

He turns his battery light on something near his foot. He goes down on his hands and knees in an excited way. He's into his bag for a little pick tool. He's picking. He sees something a little further away. He goes on his hands and knees. Picks again.

There's a roaring. There's water rising from all over.

Patchy's up to his waist in water and foam. He's wading, holding up something he's dug out of the floor of the cave. He's trying to show it to me. The water goes in his mouth—pours and gurgles and foams over his head...

There's somebody visiting down in the kitchen. I'm drifting in and out, shaking with the dream of Patchy drowned.

I'm swimming in half asleep and half awake. There's two people it sounds like down in the kitchen besides my mother and my father, talking quiet.

I'm swimming into mostly awake.

Now there's somebody else coming in from the cold. Must be a man, stomping feet. The voice is Mickey McGuire Jr.'s voice. Mickey's got a big voice and big feet. Now the voices are quiet again.

I get up and put on my frilly nightgown my mother made for me only last year, was it? It's getting a bit tight on me. I'm quiet on the stairs on purpose. I sit on the landing. Why are they talking so quiet? Fuzzy McCrank, my mother, and Frank McCrank, my father, do not normally talk quiet, specially if there's guests in the house. And Mickey McGuire Jr. is not exactly a shy flower himself.

I peek out the little landing window into the yard. There's Patchy's horse and rig there. Patchy's here! Oh, Patchy, y'er alive! Not drowned. I know that, anyway. What's the matter with me? A dream is only a dream.

Now can you believe it, here comes a car. It's Mayor Even Steven's car and he blows the horn and my father goes out without his coat only his hat and there's a short chat there with the two of them with the mayor not getting out. Then my father says thank you and the car pulls away and my father comes back in stomping the snow off. Stomping the floor. Men stomp. Women don't stomp.

I'll go down now. I can smell the pork rinds fryin'.

They're not saying a word when I come in the kitchen. What's goin' on?

"I saw your rig out there, Mr. Drizzle. Good morning to ya! And hello, Mickey. What brings you here so early?" Mickey looks at my mother. They all do.

There's a hot cup of tea in my hands already. Something's wrong. Something's bad.

My mother: "Mary Ann Alice. There's bad news. Young Jackie Boyle is dead. Killed. Killed at the dam site. Electrocuted!"

15

Chickadees and Nuthatches

MARY Ann Alice! Mary Ann Alice! The bell at St. Martin's rings muffled for Jackie Boyle.

Chickadees. You can hear the little drum of their wings. They're bold little things, these chickadees. And their cousins, the nuthatches. Almost as bad. The way they roller-coaster in and almost land on Father Foley's gown but they don't and then they dart off, up and down, flying their little roller-coasters. Their wings make a little sound of a drum. Thrrump! Thrrump!

Mary Ann Alice, Mary Ann Alice whispers the bell and thrrump thrrump go the wings of the chickadees and the nuthatches for Jackie Boyle.

The Boyles, they're a huge family and they've all gathered on the other side of the grave where Father Foley is and they're all dressed up in their best to hear Father Foley's mass prayer for the dead.

Jackie Boyle's coffin sits along the open grave in the snow with all the wreaths and gifts around.

Patchy told us the chickadees and their cousins the nuthatches go for bright colors and you can see that he's right because Father Foley has his bright red sash over his white and gold robe with the silver embroidery.

There's hundreds of people here. Great-uncle Ronald's big family and the O'Malley girls. Everybody from Low and up and down the river and dozens of the men from the dam site who didn't go home this Sunday like they usually do to their villages but stayed over for Jackie Boyle.

And there's Doobie Noonan over there standing near Andy Ryan.

And going through my head is everything they've all said about Jackie Boyle today and yesterday and even the day before about what a nice polite young man he was and how courteous he was to his elders and what a good worker he was and all the little kind things they remember him doing for people and how generous he was and how he'd make them laugh he was so funny and how much they're all going to miss him.

And how lately all he ever talked about was the piles of treasure and riches that he knew about that were hidden buried deep in the caves above the falls and how he was going to find it all and be rich as that king that came to visit at the picnic.

And how now that he was finished with school and was starting out on his own with his first real job, he liked working on the dam site so much and how interested he was in electricity and how he was going to be an electrical man later in life and that everything was going to be rosy from now on and now this terrible accident had to happen to cut him off young like that.

Father Foley is chanting and brushing away with the back of his hand a chickadee, waving it away from his head like you would bat at a summer fly.

"Chick-a-dee-dee-dee!" says the chickadee for Jackie Boyle. "Me too, me too, me too!" says the nuthatch.

And now Father Foley is finished and now they lift and now they lower Jackie into the hole while the bell sings out my name and the birds flutter around picking at the wreaths and tributes in the snow and everybody slowly leaves the churchyard.

And I feel so low because I'm trying to say to myself that I'm sad and I'll miss him and that I really did like him in spite of how I treated him but I can't. It's a lie. I didn't like him and I don't think I'll miss him. But everybody else is saying that they liked him and they'll miss him.

And now I even feel lower because everybody knows how mean and cruel to Jackie Boyle I was and how I set him up to so much laughter and ridicule because I was born so much smarter than he was. Quicker with my words and with my brain.

What will everybody think of me now?

What kind of a soul of a poet is that?

Maybe I am a cruel and a mean person.

Quicker with my words and with my brain than he was or ever would be. Not his fault.

At home, at the kitchen table, I'm sitting there with my father after the funeral.

"The lads at the dam site are all saying that young Jackie Boyle was always poking his nose in to where he was told not to. He shouldn't have been working around there where it was so dangerous. They're saying he was there after his shift when he shouldn't have been, fiddling around with something he was trying to invent that would find treasure, can you believe! Grabbed the wrong rod. Took enough of the juice to kill twenty strong men! A quick and painless way to go, my dear Mary Ann Alice. Don't you feel bad. If it didn't happen to Jackie this way it would happen to him some other way. Don't you fret!"

My father. I'm hoping he gives me one of his jokes to help me over. But he doesn't.

It's time for bed. I don't want to dream anymore. I want to sleep.

I pull the blankets to my chin. Now there's a little knock and the lamp flickering. My father, through my half open door: "You know I was talking to Father Foley only this afternoon and you won't believe what he revealed to me. He's found out that the big chief engineer himself at the dam site is in love with one of the O'Malley girls but the engineer just can't tell which one it is. He's going to have to run away with the two of them."

All the big shots at the dam site are all well dressed and snappy in their outfits. All except the big chief engineer himself. I can see him now. His hat's on crooked and his pants don't fit. One of the braces holding up his pants is attached with a pin and his boots are turned up at the toes. His coat's too small, the sleeves are too short. His hands hang down so that the bones of each wrist are the first things you see. Him and the old twins? My father. How does he come up with these yarns?

It's not one of his best ones but it's good enough to get me to go to sleep.

And not to dream, I hope.

Part II

1

Lannigan's Little Lawyer

I
T's spring, almost summer, and school is out early because of the blasting.

It's hard to be in school when things are falling off the walls.

We've spent most of the winter taking dams with Patchy and there's nothing we don't know about dams. I know more about dams than most of my hundred lads who are right there working on one.

The By-Pass is finished and our river is roaring through it whether it likes it or not. The coffer dam is in place and there's not a drop of water coming over the Paugan Falls. What they said has come true. The falls have disappeared.

"The falls is dry," says Lannigan, one of my hundred lads. He's the strongest one working on the whole dam site. He eats as much as the rest of them at his table put together.

Patchy has explained what a coffer dam is. A coffer dam is a monstrous box, a lot like the shape of a coffin but without the lid. It's made of steel and concrete and it's set down in the narrow channel above the falls on an angle to force the river into the By-Pass.

A coffer—a coffin.

The whole idea reminds me of Jackie Boyle. I miss him a bit now and I'm glad I do. It shows, maybe, that I'm not as mean a person as I thought.

Now they're blasting, on the other side of the falls, a spillway. It'll be like the hole in the top of your sink. The sink will fill up but it won't flow over. Patchy is a good explainer.

And another thing this spring. There's always lawyers around.

There's a couple of lawyers in here today as a matter of fact, eating their dinner with the men. My hundred lads aren't the Rocks in the Box Gang any more. Now they're mixing and pouring cement for the real dam itself. Now they're the Cement Heads.

The lawyers look funny sitting there. They look like they aren't invited.

They're picking at their food like birds.

The fuel today we're having is corned beef and cabbage. Tons of it. And bread and butter and tea.

One lawyer, the bald-headed one, is sitting at table four with a Cement Head named Algonquin Art.

He's from Maniwaki. He's an Algonquin. Algonquin Art.

Algonquin Art knows my Gatineau River better than anybody. He's been up and down it hundreds of times in his canoe when he was a trapper a long time ago. He's too old now for canoeing but he loves talking about the river.

When he starts you can't stop him.

He's telling the bald-headed lawyer who's sitting beside him all about the river.

Words pour out of Algonquin Art's mouth like water out of a spout.

"...above the Paugan Falls has so many twists and turns and little waterfalls comin' into it and so many tiny rapids and bits of eddies and slopes and vanishing dips and cute small pools and secret twists and funny jumps and corkscrews and runs and baby whirlpools and holes and calm stretches and half turns and dipsy doodles and it'll play so many tricks on you it'd make your head spin..."

I love to hear Algonquin Art tell about my beautiful river.

He has a little trick he plays on people sometimes. Specially strangers. He'll ask you a question and when you answer it, you're always wrong. As soon as you answer the question, he slaps his hand on the table and yells out WRONG! and laughs his head off and then asks you another question.

It's like a little play on a stage with two people in it. He's playing his play now with the bald-headed lawyer. Except the bald-headed lawyer doesn't know he's in a play.

Algonquin Art

...and then you come to a lovely little falls they call Old Lady Lyin' Down Falls. It's just a pretty little falls comin' into the river. Do you know why they call it Old Lady Lyin' Down Falls?

Bald-headed Lawyer

No, I'm afraid I don't.

Algonquin Art

Take a guess, why don'tcha?

Bald-headed Lawyer

All right. I'd imagine that it must be because the mountain ridge from which the falls proceeds has the shape of an old lady lying down.

Algonquin Art

Wrong! [*Slap table, laugh head off*] It's because one time some trappers came by there one day and there was an old lady lyin' down near there havin' a rest! I'm surprised you didn't get that one, a smart fella like you, being a lawyer and all that! [*Laugh head off again*] Now, here's one for ya! See if you can get this one. The next place you come to on the river is called Shut Your Trap Rapids. Now, why do you think it's called that?

Bald-headed Lawyer

I suppose it has some relation to the fur trade and the trapping of beaver and muskrat in the old days.

Algonquin Art

Wrong! [*Slap table, laugh head off*] It's because there was an old geezer used to live in a shack there with his wife who would never stop talking from morning till night. And whenever anybody went by they'd always hear him yelling at her, "Shut yer trap! Shut yer trap!" [*Laugh head off again*] You're not too smart are ya? Now, try this one.

Further down the river there's the Don't You Know Narrows. Why do you think it's called that?

Bald-headed Lawyer

Because nobody knows the name of the narrows?

Algonquin Art

Wrong! [*Slap table, laugh head off*] Doncheno! Doncheno! Doncheno is the native word, the Algonquin for narrows! [*Laugh head off again*] Don't ya know? Try this one. There's a place on the river we call Creek Falls. Why is it called Creek Falls?

Bald-headed Lawyer [*Giving up*]

Because a man named creek fell down there once?

Algonquin Art

Wrong! [*Slap table, laugh head off*] Creek Falls because it does! Why is there a place called Niagara?

Bald-headed Lawyer [*Giving up*]

Because there's a large falls there?

Algonquin Art

Wrong! [*Slap table, laugh head off*] Because there's nothing there at all! It's a joke! The river's as flat as yer plate along there! Here's one. Choppy Eddy. Why Choppy Eddy?

Bald-headed Lawyer

Because there's a small whirlpool or eddy there which makes the water choppy?

Algonquin Art

Wrong! [*Slap table, laugh head off*] It's because there was a lumberjack named Eddy around there who chopped wood all the time! Y'er not too smart, are ya?...

I go back in the kitchen for more food. Even from in here you can hear Algonquin Art slapping the table and laughing his head off probably asking the bald-headed lawyer about some of the other lovely places along the river that'll soon be all drowned away like Gurgle, Ripple, White Horses, Sluice, Cascade Spout, Drip and Dribble, Percolate, Gush and Flush, Chute and Cataract and Splash—all gone soon.

The other lawyer, the smaller of the two, is sitting beside Lannigan. Lannigan has a whole string of first names but nobody ever uses them. Not even himself. He's just Lannigan. He's the strongest man anybody has seen around here or heard of around here, except in songs. My father told me he was driving a streetcar down in Hull before he came to work on the dam.

One day, it was Christmas Eve, the streetcar was jammed with people and parcels. You couldn't get one more passenger on it was so crowded. The streetcar slid on some ice and came off the track. Lannigan got out and, with it loaded down like that, lifted the whole works, tram and people and parcels, back on the track with his bare hands!

Lannigan is shaking hands with the lawyer. Introducing himself. One of his fingers is bigger than this lawyer's arm. The lawyer looks like he's going to be sick.

"I don't think he's ever smelled boiled cabbage before," says Mrs. Kealey to me. We're standing there watching this lawyer and Lannigan.

"He'd better watch himself," says Mrs. Kealey, "or Lannigan might eat him by mistake."

These lawyers are up and down the river talking to farmers. Official business. They've been up to the Corks and beyond.

The little lawyer beside Lannigan has his shiny leather briefcase set down right beside him on the bench. Right close to him. Every now and then he puts his arm around it and draws it closer to himself.

Like Mickey McGuire Jr. does to me when we're sitting on the swing watching the moon come up.

It's times like that I feel like leaning closer and kissing Mickey. But I don't. It's not that I'm afraid. It's just that every time I'm like that I start to think about writing something and then the feeling of kissing him goes away.

When Lannigan eats there's liable to be quite a lot of juice flying around. The little lawyer's getting splashed pretty good with corned beef and cabbage and butter. His face is starting to look a bit green. There's tea sprayed all over his suit.

"Oh, my God!" says Mrs. Kealey. "He's going to faint!"

Sure enough, down he goes, face down in his plate. Lannigan scoops him up in one arm and gets up and carries him over to us.

"Where do you want him? He seems to be ready for a bit of a nap," says Lannigan.

"Take him over to the hospital with the O'Malley girls there. They'll take care of him," Mrs. Kealey tells him and out the door he goes. He's carrying the lawyer under his arm like a sack of washing.

Nobody's paying any attention to the briefcase sitting there by itself now and nobody sees me pick up the briefcase and carry it back into the cookhouse and hide it behind the flour bin.

2
Thief

AFTER the lads all belch and blow and cough and smoke cigarettes and fart, they leave for their long afternoon of cement.

Then we get the mess sloshed away and everything goes quiet. Now I make a little hideout behind the barrels of molasses and lard and salted fish.

What was it Mr. Cork said? He'd love to take a peek into one of them fancy briefcases of theirs?

Well, Mr. Cork. Here we go.

The snap on the briefcase is silver. There's gold initials, W.D. The leather is soft and smooth and black and shiny. You love the feel of it. It's smooth as the skin of a newborn pig. I'm thinking of Grampa Cork looking at one of these up on his farm and thinking about New York City. Then signing some paper or other.

Is this stealing? I don't think so. I'm only borrowing it for a while. While the little lawyer is taking his nap. Father Foley would say it's wrong. Wrong to snoop into business that you have no business snooping in. Well, that's all right. What Father Foley doesn't know won't hurt him now, will it? That's what I always say.

The briefcase opens almost all on its own.

Inside there's dozens of folders. Each folder has a blue tag sticking up with a name printed on. I know almost every name. Names of farms along the river. Mahoney. That's Mean Hughie's. Noonan. That's Doobie. O'Rourke. That's Great-uncle Ronald's. O'Connor. That's Mayor Even Steven's. McCrank. That's us. McGuire. That's Mickey's place. And on and on.

There's one tag sticking up that's not blue. It's red. It says *CORK*. I pull out the folder. There's a big stamp on the cover. It says FILE CLOSED. I open it. There's a stamp on the top. It says, CONFIDENTIAL. The letter is to dear somebody at the International Paper Company and Gatineau Power Corporation. The letter is signed by William Davenport. W.D.

Here's what it says:

The Cork family has no resource to pursue any land claim and their land deed is non-existent. Legally, they are squatters.

They have, for all intents and purposes, unlike most of the others, caved in already.

We will not hear anything more from the Cork family as they are sick and poor.

I have therefore closed the file. They will be officially advised to move and will, unfortunately, receive no remuneration.

Then there's a small paper attached to the letter. The paper says this:

The Cork farm, unfortunately unique on the river, has an elevation such that will result in the complete inundation of the land claimed, including all buildings. When the dam is finally shut, the whole Cork homestead will disappear forever under 12 fathoms of flood water.

I fold the letter and attached paper and slip it in the breast pocket of my apron. I pat it safe. I'm a thief.

I take out the McCrank folder. It's only a few papers. No letter signed by W.D. I pull out Noonan. It's the same. Just papers. Documents. No letter from W.D. I look at a few more. McGuire, O'Rourke. I notice they all say NEGOTIATIONS OPEN. All except the red one. The Cork one. FILE CLOSED.

I'll talk to my father about this. And Patchy.

The folders are back in where they belong and the briefcase is closed and nicely shut, thank you very much.

I take it over to the hospital through the dust and explosions and the roar of the rock crushers and hammers and drills and the lads shouting and the steam screaming and the wheels grinding and the pulleys squealing and the thunder of falling rock and the banging of the work train and the thunking of the conveyor belts. There's gas engines and steam engines and electric engines and horse engines and man engines. All to tame the river. To build a dam.

The hospital is away too small. It's always packed with people. It's only two rooms. A big room and a little one and some toilets. There's only four beds. They have a sign up over the door. "This is our _____ accident-free day." There's supposed to be a number in the blank space. But there never is. It never says "tenth" or "fourth" or even "second."

That's because there's an accident at the dam site just about every day. Maybe it's only a broken thumb or maybe it's a broken leg or worse. And there's hundreds of scratches and bruises and cuts and rips.

The O'Malley girls and the doctor are busier than bee-keepers when I go in.

The O'Malley girls have all their old remedies going. Hot bear grease and goose grease. Horseradish leaves to soak your feet. Onions stewed in molasses for all kinds of pulled muscles and bruises. Wood ashes and water stirred. Drink it for a bang on the head. Warm honey baked in a jar inside a loaf of bread poured in your ears for infection or deafness from explosions.

The doctor and his assistant are doing the bigger jobs. Sewing up gashes, putting casts on broken bones, taping up cracked ribs, tying splints on fingers, knitting up heads.

Over in the corner, the lawyer is propped up looking pretty pale but he's awake. I go over and hold out the brief-case. Is he looking at my apron? He hasn't taken the brief-case yet.

"Here's your briefcase. You forgot it in the mess hall." He still hasn't taken it.

"What are ya starin' at?" I say. He's looking a little gray around the gills

"Thank you," he says and takes the briefcase and hugs it. "Have you lived around here all your life?" he asks.

Let me tell you something. One time a farm machinery salesman came to our house to talk to my father. Soon after they started talking the salesman says to my father, "Have you lived here all your life?" Right away my father says, "Not yet!" The salesman bursts out laughing right away. After the salesman left my father told me that if anybody ever asks you if you've lived here all your life you answer "Not yet." If the person laughs right away, you can be sure that person has a quick wit and quite a few brains. If the person doesn't get the joke right away or not at all you can be sure they're probably pretty slow upstairs in the brain department.

"I beg your pardon?" I say to the lawyer.

"Have you lived here all your life?" asks the lawyer.

"Not yet!" I say.

The lawyer's face is blank as a wall of marble.

There's a long silence. He doesn't get it. Not too quick upstairs in the brain department, I guess.

"You're a very pretty girl," he says. "Do people often tell you that?"

"Every day," I say, "people smarter than you tell me that. Now, you better pack up and get on your way before Lannigan gets back and gobbles you up for a little snack!"

3

Only a Rumor

ITELL my father about what I said to the lawyer and he laughs and hugs me and tells me that he's proud of me.

Then I show the letter to my father. I tell him how I got it.

He reads it over and over. "Lawyers," he keeps saying. And reads again and again. "Lawyers." He pounds the kitchen table with his fist, making the lamp jump. I've never seen him like this. So mad.

"Mary Ann Alice," he says to me, his eyes burning. "Nobody is to know you took this letter. Nobody. Do you hear me? You are in great danger. Lawyers are powerful, powerful people. If they ever find out you stole from them they'll come and hurt you. Hurt us. Nobody is to know. Not your mother. Not your teacher. Not your priest. Not your friends. Not your neighbors. Nobody. Do you hear? Not a living soul!"

"Not even Patchy Drizzle?"

"I said *nobody!*"

"We have to tell the Corks."

"We can warn the Corks. We can try to help the Corks. But nobody is to know anything about this piece of paper!"

My father gets up and throws the letter and the paper attached into the stove.

"Nobody!"

After a while he calms down a little. He takes up my hands.

"We can say we heard. We heard a rumor. But we don't know where it came from. We can't know. Somebody said that somebody said…we heard tell that…"

He calms down some more.

"You see, Mary Ann Alice, all the farmers have some kind of deed or proof or paper proving that they own their land or at least they think they do and they're all fighting—*we're* all fighting—to make sure our proofs are good enough. None of us have caved in and signed anything saying that we don't own our own land. Except Grampa Cork. He must have signed something, not knowing what it was. Now they've closed the Cork file. A red tag. File closed. It's a terrible thing." My father looks more serious than I've ever seen him.

"You're a brave girl, my girl. But you know nothing about any letter!"

"What about the Corks?" I say. "What's going to happen to them? What will they do?"

"After the rumor gets round, we'll take a trip up to the

Corks and talk to them. See what can be done. How we can help." My father's thinking hard.

I've already decided to try out the "rumor" on Patchy Drizzle first thing tomorrow morning.

4

An Apology and Green from Blue

Y hundred lads, fifty at a time, the Cement Heads, are eating porridge, pork and beans, bread and tea for breakfast.

Lannigan likes to eat for a while then rest. While he's resting he fills his mouth with tea and sloshes it around in there and then you hear a big swallow.

Mrs. Kealey says the sound of the tea moving around in Lannigan's mouth reminds her of somebody rinsing out a barrel.

After clean-up I stroll into town and head up to Patchy's house.

You can hear the rumble at the dam site from here. Patchy said once it sounds like the sounds he heard when he was in the war.

I don't mind knocking on Patchy's door now.

Mrs. Drizzle and I aren't enemies anymore.

It's because of what happened last Christmas Eve.

Last Christmas Eve was a special night for somebody

lucky or unlucky enough to have the soul of a poet like me.

The night was mild—mild and not a cloud in the sky. All day there were clouds and fat flakes fell soft but piled up to no more than the length of your thumb in goose down on the ground.

Mickey McGuire Jr. wanted to come with us in the buggy to midnight mass at St. Martin's but I told him I'd see him there at the church and that I wanted to be alone. He took on a hurt look when I told him that but he shouldn't have felt bad. It's just I wanted to be by myself. Nothing against him. I like being with Mickey. But I like being alone sometimes, too.

My mother and father, Fuzzy and Frank, were going with the horse and rig or maybe Mayor Even Steven would come over in his car because he's got nobody, he's not married and lives alone and likes to be with us to go on special occasions.

But I wanted to walk. It's a half hour or more to walk, depending if you stop on the road to look into the dark bush or at the starlight across the blue-black fields or to lean way back and take in all of the Christmas sky without a winter cloud in it anywhere and without falling over backwards while you're at it.

My father understood it better than the others. He'd been down blowin' his bugle by the river lately, I'd noticed.

He likes to be alone sometimes, too.

That night I was dressed up.

When they canceled the dance at the covered bridge at Low last year my mother canceled the dress she was making for it and instead made me a new set of clothes.

I've got a pleated wool skirt, tight at the waist and flared out at the shins. Nobody has one but me. When I spin round it swirls out. It's a light green shade. My stockings are Argyle, the diamond shapes are different shades of green. My blouse is frilly at the neck and long sleeved with pearl buttons down the front and on the wrists. It's a dark green. My hair is tied up at the back with a green ribbon and a tail hanging. I have a green kerchief for a hat for church. I have small shoes to put on when I take off my boots. The shoes are green.

That night everything I had on, except my underwear, was green.

My skirt has a deep side pocket. In it I had a bit of licorice for my breath and Patchy's hammer he gave me. I carry it around in case I see a rock face along the road I want to give a tap to. The hammer is heavy and solid but only small—the size of one of Mr. and Mrs. Cork's clay pipes.

I was on the Martindale road in the quiet and the stars. The snow fluffed up around my ankles like feathers. I was thinking of Mrs. Drizzle. How lonely she was and how nasty I was to her. I was thinking of how I would apologize to her. The words I would use when the time came.

On the crest of the road in front of me there was somebody coming toward me. A figure hooded. Closer now. Soon I saw part of her face in the starlight.

It was Mrs. Drizzle! I hadn't seen her since that day. It was magic. My thoughts made this happen.

"Good evening, Mrs. Drizzle," I said. "It's me, Mary Ann Alice McCrank."

"Oh, dear," she said. "I didn't expect—"

"I was just thinking about you," I said. "Can you believe it often happens to me? I'll think of something and suddenly there it is?"

"Mary Ann Alice McCrank, I have thought of you, too. May I apologize for my behavior that day? I behaved abominably. And doubly so since you were a guest in my home." She pulled her hood back. Her long face was pale and sad in the starlight.

"I've been wanting to say I was sorry to you for what I said about your name," I said. "Often my mouth makes me ashamed of myself."

"You're going to church, aren't you?" she said.

"Yes. Where are you headed?

"I don't know."

"Would you come with me?"

"Oh, I don't know if—"

"We could sit at the back. You wouldn't have to do anything. The music will be lovely. We have a lovely choir. You don't have to care about the prayin' part. You could skip that. A lot of people do."

"No, I think not. I will walk back with you, though. It's a wondrous night."

We walked together. The black trees and tall rocks moved across the sky with all the stars.

"Do you have nights like this in England?" I said. My voice didn't sound like my own voice.

"No, we do not. Nothing like this. So many stars. This is another world. The snow. The warmth of the cold. The gothic trees like church spires. In moments like these," she said, "I see why you all love this land."

"It's all we have," I said.

At the church we said goodnight. She touched my arm. I watched her in her hood so lonesome go down the road toward Low through the feathers, through the spruce trees stabbing up into the stars.

Mickey McGuire Jr. was in our pew with my mother and father waiting for me. I took off my coat and boots so that everybody would notice my new green outfit when I got up to take communion.

Father Foley's sermon was about how God created the whole world only four thousand and four years ago and then about shepherds and wise men and the Virgin Mary and the stable and the baby Jesus.

While Father Foley was talking, Mickey edged closer and whispered in my ear. "Yer blue clothes look lovely on ya, Mary Ann Alice." You could hear him whispering all over the church with that voice of his.

Blue? Blue! Did he say blue?

While he was saying this he put his hand on my knee.

I fished out the little geology hammer from my deep pocket and gave him a quick snap of a rap on the fingers that would have split a chunk of gneiss in two. Father Foley stopped talking and looked down to see what all the racket was.

"Jaysus!" said Mickey McGuire Jr., pulling away his hand and stuffing it between his legs for the pain.

5

Dam Lies

MRS. Drizzle opens the door.

She starts talking right away about the town near where she was born called Wakefield. And about how the church cathedral there took two hundred years to build and was finished in the year 1300. And how big and high it is.

"Your church, Mary Ann Alice, in Martindale is a lovely little church but I have to tell you that you could put your church *inside* the cathedral in the town of Wakefield in the middle of England and it would disappear!" Sip.

She doesn't mean to be mean about it. She's just lonesome.

I tell her that I'd like to go there and see that sometime. She doesn't answer.

"Do you think you'll ever go back for a visit?" I say.

"Not very likely," she says. "If I did go, I'd never come back here. I'd stay there. But I can't do that. A promise is a promise. I made my choice. You make your choice and you live with it. That's life. The Wakefields always keep their word. The Wakefields never break a promise. 'Till death do us part' we said in the big cathedral over there in Wakefield. That was the vow."

There is no more to say.

There's another blast way down at the Spillway. You can feel it through your legs. The earth's crust is like a drum, Patchy told us once. Or a string on a harp. It carries vibrations like musical notes.

"Mr. Drizzle is out the back with his rocks," she tells me.

I go round the back and there's Patchy, standing there like a photograph. He's got his hands in his pockets. He's looking down toward his feet. His head is away over on the side. You've never seen anybody sadder looking.

We talk a bit about rocks and I get around to mentioning about a rumor going around. About flooded farms. Especially about the Cork farm.

Patchy surprises me. How much he already knows.

All the farms along the river will be affected. Some will lose very little, some whole fields. Most of the farmers will be compensated if they show any kind of documents of ownership. There are two farms, though, that will suffer terrible loss. Mean Hughie will lose over half his fields. The Cork farm will disappear completely.

"How do you know this?" I say.

"All you have to do is look," says Patchy. "Look at the elevations. The dam will raise the water 30.4 meters. That's engineering talk for exactly 100 feet. That's about twice as high as your bell in the church. I'm going up the river this afternoon. If you want to come with me, I'll show you."

I run back through the explosions and yelling men and crashing and falling rocks and dirt and the grinding of machines, like a war so Patchy said, at the dam site. Part of the dam is finished. The top of it is as wide as a narrow road. There's a big cheer goes up. Somebody has to take a team of horses and a wagon of supplies out to the end along the top of the dam.

They've picked the best man with the best team to go out.

It's Andy Ryan. From down here at mess hall number one it'd make you dizzy looking way up there. Andy Ryan's team look about the size of horseflies up there pulling a little wagon made of toothpicks. Across the top to the end.

There's no guard rails.

If the dynamiting scares the horses…

Doobie Noonan can't look. She's got her face in her hands.

Andy Ryan and his team start out across the narrow top of the dam toward the first pier. It's certain death if he goes over the side. Everybody below is holding their breath.

A deafening blast sends dust and lumps of dirt and rocks sky high so's you can't see Andy Ryan and his team anymore. Where are they? Are they all right? We have to wait.

Doobie peeks out through her fingers. She shuts them again.

Out the other side of the dirt and dust cloud comes Andy. He's safe! He's made it to the pier! Everybody gives another big cheer—you can look now, Doobie—only a bigger one this time.

Andy Ryan is a hero!

I get Mrs. Kealey to get another girl to take my place for dinner and supper and in no time Patchy and I are in his rig heading up to my place.

My father comes out to greet us.

"Patchy's going up the river and I'm going with him. He's going to show me how high the water's comin' up. Some farms are going to disappear," I tell him.

"Heard rumors, have you?" says my father to Patchy.

"Whatever you may have heard," says Patchy, "is true. Will you come with us?"

All the way up the river, while we're fighting the current and dodging the rapids, Patchy shows us how.

"Look anywhere on the shore. Now, in your imagination, place St. Martin's Church there. Now, double the height. That's where the water will be."

Going by Mean Hughie's farm it's easy to see that he's going to lose more than half of it. Pile two Martindale churches on his shore. The water will be halfway to his house.

"And I don't think he has any papers. He won't get paid a red cent." That's all my father can say. He's puffing too hard from the rowing.

We glide into the calm pool in front of the Cork farm.

I squint my eyes and place St. Martin's Church right

on Cork wharf. Now I double it.

It takes my breath away. The whole Cork farm will disappear. The water will rise about to the top of the high sheer cliff at the back of the farm.

Mr. Cork comes through the field to meet us.

My father doesn't waste any time.

He tells Mr. Cork that he's pretty sure and so's everybody else that the water's going to cover him up completely and that he better start getting ready to move and that unless he has some kind of paper or other showing he actually owns the land he won't get a red cent for it.

For a long time we stand there in the low field.

At last, Mr. Cork:

"I don't believe it. It's only rumors. It's not going to come up that high. Not this far up the river. Down the river maybe. But not this far."

Patchy tells him again what my father said only in a different way.

"It's not true," says Mr. Cork. "We're not moving. The lawyer said it's going to be all right. He said he'd check again but he thought it was probably going to be all right. The water would come up some. But not that much. He said he'd look into it. And the deed. He said we might not need a deed. He'd see about it. We're stayin'. We're not moving. It's going to be all right."

My head is getting hot.

"What lawyer told you that?" I say, real innocent. My father gives me a look with a warning in it.

"Fella come up here a week or more ago. Nice enough

lad. Fer a lawyer, anyway." My father's staring at me.

"What'd he look like?" I say, even more innocent. My father's glaring at me.

Patchy's wondering what's going on.

"Little fella. Nice clothes. Lovely briefcase with him. W.D. written right on the leather. Pure gold it looked like."

We stand around a bit more.

I've said more than enough. My father's about to come over and clap his hand over my mouth. Mr. Cork says some more. "Tried to get him to come into the house and have a cuppa tea and maybe show the briefcase to Grampa Cork but he got looking a little worried and said he'd come in the next time, the next time he was by, but not now because he had appointments and he was in a big hurry. Busy man, I guess. Important man..."

My head feels like it's on fire.

6

Cement

M Y father has figured out why the little lawyer is such a liar. And why all of them are going to be lyin' to all of us in one way or another from now on until this is all over and the water is up and we're all half drowned.

It's because they're afraid. They're afraid to go on a farm and tell the farmer any bad news. They're afraid because of what Mean Hughie did last year to his lawyer. Frightened him almost to death by putting him on the sawhorse and threatening to separate his head from the rest of his body with the buck saw.

Now you hardly see any of them around anymore. And you can't get anybody around to tell you anything about anything. Only letters now and then that hardly anybody can understand and when they finally do get them figured out the letters don't seem to say anything anyway.

Doobie Noonan comes running into the cookhouse today so worked up we think she's being chased by the police. Her mind isn't on lawyers or dams.

"I got to cut Andy Ryan's hair today," she says, tripping over her breath.

She tells us that while he was in the chair she thought he looked at her in the big mirror and even said something to her! She got so excited, she says, that she nearly cut off his ear.

She says his head is so lovely she nearly fainted.

She kept his hair in an envelope, she tells me.

Andy Ryan makes six trips a day out on the dam with his team. He's famous. The men at the dam site make twenty cents an hour. Andy Ryan makes sixty cents an hour. Because of his team of wonderful horses and because he's so good and brave. He's getting rich, he is, with this enormous pay.

Patchy is more and more in the caves this summer and less and less at home and Mrs. Drizzle (Victoria, I almost call her now) is more and more alone.

My father is going to try to raise money for the Cork family in case they change their minds and decide to move. He's visited them a dozen times but they won't budge.

"Old man Cork," my father says, "is like a dog with a stick!"

The dam gets higher and stronger. It's hard to believe there's so much cement in this world. The dam gets longer and longer.

The lads come in for supper and their overalls are stiff with cement.

Lannigan doesn't wear overalls. Just his pants. When he comes in and sits down to eat, his pants explode they're so caked in cement.

Up the river, Mr. Cork is piling a stone wall on the low part of his shoreline along where his wharf is. He says it will keep the water out from the lower part of his field. That way he won't lose any ground at all. Also he comes down to our place twice a week, often at night, to see if there's any mail for him from the little lawyer.

You can hear the Corks coming down the river in the summer moonlight and in the sound of the crickets, the squeaky oar squeakin' and the bailing can scraping.

Is there any mail? No, Mr. Cork. There never is and there never will be.

7

Priceless

PATCHY Drizzle has found the buried treasure that he's been talking about. It's not the kind of treasure that poor Jackie Boyle thought was down there in the caves. It's not gold or jewels or diamonds or money that Jackie must have been thinking about. It's not a chest of stolen gems hid there by pirates that poor Jackie must have been rolling around in his dreams.

The dreams that killed him.

No, it's something more valuable. Something so valuable that you can't put a price on it. It's priceless.

It's a perfect fossil of an arthropod. A long dragonfly. About the length of the little hammer Patchy gave me. A fossil is the outline in solid rock of an ancient animal. An arthropod is any invertebrate with jointed legs and a segmented body. An invertebrate is any creature that has no backbone. I got an A in the test. I wonder what it would be like not to have a backbone.

I asked my father. He said why don't you ask the little

lawyer the next time you see him. He'll know for sure how it feels.

Patchy has no doubt whatsoever how old this dragonfly is.

Hang on to yer hats!

The dragonfly is three hundred million years old!

The rumor about the fossil is all around and everybody is curious. People see Patchy on the street and they stop him and ask him if they could see it sometime. At church they ask Patchy about it. Because of the way rumors always get things mixed up and wrong the questions they ask sometimes seem awful stupid.

"This ol' t'ing ya found, is it still alive at all?"

"I suppose it smells terrible, does it?"

"I hear it's as big as a horse. What would a horse be doin' way down there? How would he get there in the first place?"

"What's the good of it if it's dead?"

"I hear tell ya found a dragon down there. Does it shoot fire out of its mouth or anything like that?"

Two days a week now, Patchy sits on his porch with it for an hour just before noon and people come by on purpose and drop up on the porch to have a peek at it.

Patchy has it nestled in a big cushion. He has one of his signs beside it. I wrote it for him. It's not one of my serious poems.

Yez've finally found me! Y'er finally awake!
Well, don't stand there gawkin'—bring on the cake!

And listen to this (hang on to yer bonnet)
Put three hundred million candles upon it!
Happy Birthday to Me,
Arthur the Arthropod.

The fossil is a perfect outline. You can even see his eye holes. His little feet. The veins in his long wings. His handsome head.

Arthur is truly beautiful.

Some people look at Arthur and screw up their noses. Others are afraid. They stay on the middle step of the porch and stand on tiptoe.

Some just shrug their shoulders.

"Sassy little fella, isn't he?" says one woman.

"Where in God's name are we gonna find three hundred million candles?" a kid says.

"And how's he gonna blow them out? Isn't he dead?" says his brother.

Great-uncle Ronald looks for the longest time. "I'm trying to imagine that much time passing, but I can't. I just can't."

One of the old O'Malley girls (we don't know which one) wonders what color Arthur was when he was alive and flying around. "We'll never know, will we?" says the other O'Malley girl. "There was nobody around to keep notes then, was there?"

Mayor Even Steven looks at it and now he wants to open a museum.

Father Foley walks right by.

"No, thank you!" he calls out. "Lovely day?"

"That's rude," I say to Patchy. "He could at least look at it."

"The Father doesn't like this kind of study. I asked him once if he wanted to join me in the caves for a visit. He said no. His field of study is in the next world. Mine is in this one." Patchy seems lost in his thoughts.

My father told me, after he saw Arthur, that Father Foley told him in all confidence that if you stared too long into the eye holes of Arthur the Arthropod, the Devil would turn you into a pillar of horse manure.

"Don't listen to him," my mother said.

While Mickey McGuire Jr. was looking at Arthur, I decided to tease him a bit. "Would you like to come with me down into the caves one afternoon and explore around? Maybe we could find another dragonfly—a friend for Arthur here."

"I suppose I might," he said. "You wouldn't be bringing that hammer of yours wit' ya, would ya?"

And now here it is July, the heat bugs are screaming, the dynamite explosions in the Spillway are getting louder and more dangerous, the dam is getting longer, the lads' overalls are so stiff with cement that when they take them off, the overalls stand there in the corner all by themselves.

And now Patchy surprises me.

He gives me Arthur the Arthropod to take home to my place and put away somewhere very safe.

"Keep him with you for as long as you want," says Patchy. "He'll make you think."

Makes me think all right.

I'm thinking why did Patchy Drizzle give his prize possession to me? Is he afraid Arthur's not safe at his own house? Is Patchy going on a trip or something?

8

The Smell of Dynamite

BREAKFAST is the best job of the three. Supper is the next best. Dinner is the worst because it's the middle of the day. Breakfast is cool and pleasant and everything feels fresh and clean. With supper the mess hall is pretty hot still but it's starting to cool down. But dinner is the hardest because of the heat of the noon sun outside and the roaring stoves and the sweating bodies inside.

Andy Ryan is eating with us now.

Mrs. Kealey has put me in charge of the three or four other girls waiting on the tables. One of my girls has quit and guess who's on my crew now?

Doobie Noonan, of course.

Soon as she heard Andy Ryan was with us she quit the barber shop and was over here in mess hall number one as quick as you can say "shave and a haircut!"

Doobie is a good worker so I had no trouble talking Mrs. Kealey into taking her on.

At breakfast the men are fairly quiet and they talk about fairly quiet things. Sometimes some of the older lads will talk about how the falls used to be. How the water was clean and clear above the falls and how you could see the fish down there against the green weeds and the white rock. And how they'd dive when they were kids off that big leaning maple, remember that tree, you'd dive into the faster water up there and head across and fight the current and just make it to the other edge before you got drawn over the falls...

Or about where the best berries are or the tastiest brook trout. Or the smell of clover in the hayfield. Or how to carve a whistle out of a willow stick. Or how Kazabazua is the Indian word for hidden waters. Or why Hull, Chelsea, Wakefield, Low, Kazabazua and Gracefield are all the same distance apart. Or how hemlock is the best tree for making railroad ties...

Or Lannigan tells how big and strong his grandfather was. When Lannigan was a kid his grandfather would get him up before dawn by going out and shaking all the trees to get the birds started. Then he'd go and slap the rooster awake and make him crow. Or he'd go out and lift the corner of the house and let it drop and knock everybody out of their beds onto the floor...

Mrs. Kealey's got ten of our biggest iron frying pans on. Seven of them are cooking pancakes and the other three are frying curled-up salty pork.

There's five tables—ten men at each table. This is the first shift of fifty lads.

There's a half-gallon can of maple syrup on each table. And platters of pancakes and fried pork.

One of Doobie's tables is the table where Andy Ryan always eats. Doobie makes sure that Andy Ryan's table gets the best platters. She puts the best cooked pancakes on the platter closest to where Andy Ryan is sitting. She has the best pancakes at one end of the platter. She turns the platter so that the end of the platter is pointing right at Andy Ryan. As soon as the platter hits the table and Doobie gives it a half turn all the forks go stabbing and, sure enough, Andy Ryan gets three of the best pancakes with one stab of his fork. Does he know she's doing this? No, he doesn't.

As a matter of fact, we think that Mr. Ryan doesn't even know Doobie exists.

Faster than you can say "pass the syrup" the platter's empty and it's time for a refill.

Mrs. Kealey is standing there with her long wooden spoon. She's watching Lannigan.

"What's wrong with Mr. Lannigan this morning?" she says. "Is he not feeling well? He's only downed two and a half platters of pancakes and a half a platter of pork. Do you think maybe we should call in the doctor? See why he's lost his appetite?"

Lannigan's got himself a new pile of pancakes you can hardly see over. He's got a gob of butter on top the size of yer fist and he's poured half the can of syrup over it all.

"We're gonna need some more syrup at this table!" one of the lads calls out.

"We're gonna need some more of just about every-thing!" another shouts.

"I wonder if they're havin' a contest, er what?" says Mrs. Kealey.

The clean-up is harder than usual because of all the frying pans we had to use and also because of the maple syrup all over the tables and down on the benches and on the floor.

There's even maple syrup on the wall behind where Lannigan was sitting this morning.

Usually there's time for a break in the middle of the morning but today there's not and my girls are groaning and whining. In the break I usually take a walk up to see if Patchy's home. But not today.

In her break, Doobie likes to read her serial story she's following in the Ottawa *Citizen* which is delivered every evening by the train. She's reading "The Gray Phantom's Romance: The Astonishing Adventures of a Lovable Outlaw." But not today.

We're having roast pork, gravy, mashed potatoes and boiled onions for dinner. It's just barely ready when the first fifty come piling in at twelve o'clock.

"What's the fuel today?" some of them are yelling.

There's dozens of cement overalls standing up all by themselves along the walls.

The lads are shoveling the roast pork and potatoes and onions down their gullets so fast that you'd think they haven't eaten in a month.

Mrs. Kealey is slicing roast pork off the five big roasts

so fast you can hardly see the knife move. It's just a blur.

The hundred-pound bag of potatoes that we peeled and boiled and mashed fills twenty big bowls. Ten for this shift, ten for the next.

Two bowls for each table. Except Lannigan's table. Three bowls there. The next shift will be a bowl short. Too bad. There'll be growling.

Everybody's talking about how Lannigan saved some lad's life over at the rock crusher. The new lad, from Mushrat, got the sleeve of his overalls caught in the gears and was being pulled into the crusher. Lannigan caught hold of the tough overall cloth and hung on to it until the machine gave up and quit. Stripped the gears, Lannigan did.

"He'd a been dead for sure, the lad from Mushrat!"

"Crushed into little pieces the size of walnuts!"

"Smaller than that. Chokecherries!"

"There would a been nuttin' left of him at all!"

"At all, at all!"

"At all, at all, at all!"

"He'd a been nothing but mush!"

"The Mush from Mushrat!"

"Have some more mashed potatoes, Lannigan!"

"Good man y' are, Lannigan, me lad! Have another bowl of boiled onions!"

"Do you have a special treat for Lannigan, here, Mrs. Kealey? He saved a lad from Mushrat from bein' turned into mush today!"

Mrs. Kealey goes into the cookhouse and brings out

one of the big roasts of pork she hasn't sliced yet. She hoists it down in front of him, roasting pan and all.

"Here!" she says, and laughing and cheering goes all around the mess hall.

Halfway through dinner the backs of the lads' shirts and under the arms are soaked in sweat. It's so hot in here you can hardly breathe. The four windows are open but there's only dead air. The more the lads eat, the hotter they get. The sweat's pouring off their foreheads and dripping into their eyes.

Mrs. Kealey's had us put a rag at each man's place. The lads are mopping their heads with the rags. The more they eat the more the sweat pours out of their pores. It's running off their heads and dripping off the ends of their noses into their food.

Some of them shake their heads and send showers of sweat along the table.

Lannigan wrings his sweat rag out onto the floor.

Mrs. Kealey is standing there, taking a rest and shaking her head.

"Mary Ann Alice," she says, "do you think it would help if we supplied each one of them with an umbrella? Or maybe bathing suits?"

Mrs. Kealey makes me laugh. I'm walking over to tell Doobie and my crew what Mrs. Kealey just said. But now I'm halfway across the mess hall on my hands and knees. A terrible explosion rocks the building and sends down pieces of the ceiling. There's rocks and dirt flying in the window. There's broken dishes and food everywhere.

The lads are tearing outside into the smoke and dust and the smell of dynamite

Outside you can't see a thing. Dirt and fumes and everything in pieces.

And thunder and shuddering.

And now shouting and running.

Mess hall number three is on fire.

There's another smaller blast. You can hear horses crying.

A lot of the lads have been hurt. None of my fifty, though. They're sending for Dr. Geggie in Wakefield and anybody else he can bring. They're shooting injured horses.

Work is stopped. There's bulldozers pushing everything that's broken into big piles.

A wagon with dynamite in it tipped over above the head of the By-Pass and blew up. The driver jumped behind a big boulder and saved himself. The horses are blown to bits. The blast went all the way up to the caves and back down the By-Pass and out the other end. Everything around was sucked down the By-Pass.

You can hardly breathe, the air is so thick with dirt and smoke and the smell of explosions and the heat.

Everybody's asking if anybody is killed. Or missing. It's a miracle that nobody's killed so far as we know. Is anybody missing? Maybe. Maybe not. Don't know for sure yet.

I walk into town away from the dam site. I go up to Patchy's house. I knock.

Mrs. Victoria Drizzle opens the door.

No, he's not here.

Left before breakfast, as usual, for his beloved caves. She says one of these days she's going to take all those rocks of his and dispose of them in the river. She says do I want to come in. She says the explosion knocked two of her valuable china plates off the wall and broke them.

I say I don't think I will and go back to the dam site.

She won't throw away his rocks. She's only in a bad mood.

I have a terrible feeling deep in my stomach.

I have the taste of iron in my mouth.

My heart is thumping away here under my shirt.

The heat of the sun feels like poison.

9

The Word

THERE'S an oilcloth on our kitchen table with a picture printed all over it like you see on wallpaper. The picture is of a farmer and his wife stooking grain in a field beside a river. Across the river is a mountain of pine trees. There are seven stooks of grain standing in the picture. The farmer is carrying two sheaves of grain and the farmer's wife is leaning over to pick up a sheaf. There are seven sheaves lying on the ground. On the river there's a rowboat with a person rowing. The picture is repeated over and over.

Ever since I was a little girl I've looked every day at this picture. And my eyes always go on to the next one and the next one even though they're all exactly the same. That's what I'm doing now.

The picture looks like our lower field and our river that we look at every day out our kitchen window.

Our lovely field that will be under water pretty soon and disappear forever.

I'm looking at the pictures repeated over and over again on the tablecloth while I tell my mother and father how they found pieces of Patchy's boat beyond the end of the By-Pass. One piece of board has part of the boat's name *The Dolomite*. The last part—omite.

I brought the board home with me. I put it in my closet with Arthur the Arthropod.

Nobody's laid eyes on Patchy all day.

Some of the lads searched along both shores below the dam site. Some of them walked into the water and even tried diving under but you can't see a thing down there there's so much churned-up mud and cement dust and foam and broken wood floating and dead fish killed by dynamite.

There were two men missing. They found one wandering down the main road toward Brennan's Hill in a daze, half stupid from a bang on the head he got in a shower of rocks.

Now there's only one missing.

This afternoon I took our boat and rowed down along the caves. I went in the first one and called out soft his name.

Near the opening of the second cave I saw something lying on the rock floor.

Patchy's geology bag. Empty.

I have the bag in my closet with Arthur the Arthropod and the piece of board that says "omite."

When the rumor got spread around that I found Patchy's bag, people started thinking thoughts that I don't want to think. A word is in people's heads but not on their lips.

Tomorrow they're going to send some divers into the water above the By-Pass and near the caves.

And they'll search every inch of the caves.

My mother and father are thinking but they're not saying.

The farmer is still carrying the two sheaves of grain on the tablecloth and the farmer's wife is still leaning over to pick up a sheaf. The person in the boat is still rowing on the river.

Logs that got sucked down the By-Pass by the explosion are splintered and smashed into toothpicks.

Nobody will say the word.

What did poor Jackie Boyle think Patchy's boat was called? Dynamite?

My father is looking very sad at me.

My mother is frowning. She's thinking of what to say to me. Don't say it.

"I hate that dam," I say so soft I can hardly hear myself.

"Mary Ann Alice, darlin', we'll all pray that Patchy Drizzle is safe," my mother says.

Then the dam behind my eyes breaks apart and I flood my face with tears.

My mother and father both get up out of their chairs and come around and hold me.

I'm blinded by my sorrow and fear.

"Patchy Drizzle is not drowned!" I cry. "He's *NOT DROWNED!*"

PART III

1

Lannigan Dines at the Cork Residence

MICKEY McGuire Jr. has quit school. He was going to be in grade eight with me but he wants to be a farmer with his dad and Great-uncle Ronald and he says it's useless to be wasting your time specially with the new teacher we have. Others have quit, too, and there's only three or four of us left in the grade depending on who decides to show up. Mickey shows up some days but it's only to bother the new teacher and to show off in front of me. He's actually quit, like I said.

I can tell that Mickey knows how I feel, Mickey does, although I never say I feel sad and sort of lost. And this new teacher we have is making things even worse.

One day, not long after school started, Mickey had an idea to go over and talk to Mr. McLaughlan at the store. "Let's go over and talk to old man McLaughlan," Mickey says. "He'll have some things to say about teachers." Mickey knew listening to Mr. McLaughlan would cheer me up a bit.

You don't feel so bad if somebody else knows you feel bad.

Mr. McLaughlan was filling and weighing small bags of white navy beans. Bags that would be a good size for a family. I wondered if he ever saw the loads of beans that we get in for fuel for the human machines at the dam site.

It didn't take us long to get him going about teachers.

"My grandfather had a cousin. Boghole Kavanagh I believe his name was. He was a teacher. Went off to Duluth, Minnesota. Going to teach people over there. Right beside his school there was a gallows. Where they'd hang people. Public hangings. Everybody'd gather around. Fun to watch, you know. Enjoyed that, they did. Put everybody in a good mood. Feelin' glad you're not up there yerself. One day, Boghole is out there with his pupils watching one. Would you believe that the man up there with the rope around his neck was a fella from Low? A distant cousin of Boghole's! Boghole shouts up, 'Danno! Is that you, Danno?' 'Boghole!' shouts the cousin. 'Bog, is that you?' 'It is,' says Boghole. 'How's everything goin'?' They're putting the black bag over the cousin's head.

"'Everything's goin' just grand,' says Danno. 'Except for this, of course!'"

Mr. McLaughlan had us laughing and I suddenly felt like kissing Mickey McGuire Jr. For coming up with such a good idea. But I couldn't very well, could I, right there in the store? Mr. McLaughlan wasn't finished.

"My mother had a cousin, Dorella Crapper. Lovely lady. She was a teacher. Wound up way down in New

Orleans. To teach them down there. What was she teaching them? I don't know what she was teachin' them. Everything they didn't know, I suppose. Always a very pleasant lady. Nice to everybody. Never cursed or yelled at her pupils. Allergic to chalk unfortunately. Started sneezing down there one day. Sneezed herself to death. Terrible thing. How's that new teacher of yours makin' out?"

Our new teacher's name is Miss Fish.

She told us the first day that her name was from the Greek word "ichthus," which was a secret code name for Jesus Christ, Son of God, Savior. Because in the olden days being a Christian was a crime they said the secret name "ichthus," which was "fish," so's nobody would know they were Christians.

I thought that first day that she was going to be an interesting teacher, but that was the first and the last interesting thing she told us.

Now everybody torments her all day and she has a hard time to get through the day and I have a real strong urge to do like Mickey did and quit.

Her two favorite subjects are the Bible and etiquette. Etiquette is the rules of manners.

She's taken everything of Patchy's down off the walls and piled it all in the storeroom. All his rocks and drawings and maps and little interesting messages and questions. The third day of school I asked her if she'd let me tidy up the storeroom for her.

When she was gone, I took all of his rock specimens and took them up and gave them to Mrs. Drizzle.

"Might as well keep them safe till he comes back?" I said. I looked into her face. Her long face had no expression. But I could read her thoughts.

She didn't believe he was ever coming back.

"I'll put them in the back shed with his other things," she said. "Thank you, Mary Ann Alice, you've been very kind."

She was wearing black.

I also took his teaching hat out of the closet. I took it home and put it with Arthur and "omite" and his empty geology bag. I put the hat in the closet very careful, like you would a baby.

At school, I feel like being mean to Miss Fish like everybody else is, even the young ones.

Some of them follow her home after school to Brook's Hotel where she's staying and taunt her.

She hates all of us, I think, and she's only been here two weeks.

She's teachin' us etiquette. Here's some:

When you are a dinner guest at someone's home and the hostess offers you a second helping of roast beef, you are supposed to say, "I've had sufficient, thank you." Whether you are still hungry or not. Whether you want some more or not.

And when you cut the roast beef with your knife and fork, your fork is in your left hand and the knife is in your right hand. You cut off a bite-sized piece. Then you put down the knife beside your plate and transfer the fork to your right hand and lift up the piece of roast beef on the fork and slip it in your mouth. You don't *STAB* the meat. And you don't open your mouth any wider than one-third of the way.

When she's telling us this I'm thinking that maybe we should try to row her up to the Corks for a little etiquette dining up there with them.

Maybe Mr. Cork would do something he did when I was there with Mickey one time. We were having a big feed of fried eggs and mostly raisin bread. A chicken flew up on the table and Mr. Cork threw a cuppa hot tea at it.

My father called it "mostly" raisin bread because some of the raisins were actually dead flies.

Would that be etiquette enough for her?

Miss Fish gave us a piece of writing to do.

The title was "Some Points on the Etiquette of Dining Out."

I wrote her a story (almost three pages) about how Lannigan was invited up to the Cork residence to "dine." (Lannigan's never been there. I made that part up.)

The story ended up there was food on the ceiling and over in Grampa Cork's spit pail. I couldn't think of a real good last sentence so I said, "And it wound up that the flies probably ate as much if not more than the people."

I got the pages of writing back from Miss Fish the next day with the letter "F" in big print on the first page. At the end of it on page three she wrote in red pencil the word "Disgusting."

She's been glaring at me ever since.

Patchy would have laughed his head off at the pages I

wrote. Looks like I haven't got the soul of a poet anymore. As far as Miss Fish is concerned anyway.

One morning about half past ten right in the middle of Miss Fish telling us about Genesis, the first book of the Bible, everybody in the schoolhouse got up and ran out. Left her there talking to herself.

We knew there was a special train comin' and we heard the whistle. There's never a train at half past ten.

Outside, everybody was running.

Almost everybody in town was heading to the station.

I'm usually there for every train these days.

There's two from Maniwaki, one in the morning, one in the afternoon; and two from Ottawa, both in the evening. I meet as many of them as I can. You never know who might arrive. Who might be getting off.

This special train was carrying thirteen huge steel plates for the dam site. They'll be the gates at the Spillway to be lifted or lowered by pulleys to control the level of the water after the flood.

Everybody is saying that once those steel plates get to Low, it won't be long before the dam is finished and the water will start to come up.

We stayed the rest of the day, until school was out, watching the steel plates being lifted off the train by big cranes.

Then I went to my job at mess hall number one to feed the Cement Heads their supper.

Everybody believes Patchy Drizzle is d—.

Except me.

2

If I Was a Tamarack Tree and a Rock Is a Clock

I'M working hard with my father cutting trees and burning brush. We're cleaning up the bush part of our land that's going to be under water. My father wants it to be clear so that the bottom will be like a real river bottom and not full of rotting trees and dead wood. Some of the other farmers think he's wasting his time. You won't be able to see what's under the water so what's the use, they say.

"I won't see it," my father says, "but I'll know it's there and that's enough for me. Just because ya can't see something doesn't mean it isn't there."

We're sitting at the table eating our supper.

"Every time I look out this window at the new high water down there, it'll bother me, all those drowned trees. Fifty times a day I'll look out this window and I'll picture each and every tree there that I know better than the back of me hand, standing tall there in the dark, drowning, never to feel the sun again."

"All right, all right," says my mother nice and soft. "Eat your supper before it's cold."

"If I was a hardwood tree I'd rather wind up burning in the stove keeping the house warm than spend the rest of me days caught there under water."

"All right, Frank, all right," says my mother.

"If I was a pine tree I'd rather wind up built into a table or a floor than spend the rest of me time covered in green slime."

"Have some more meat, Frank," says my mother.

"If I was a spruce or a balsam I'd sooner be floated down to the mill in Hull and be crushed up and turned into pages of a newspaper, say, the New York *Times* with a picture of Lindbergh the first man to fly alone across the ocean stamped on me than live out the rest of me time on earth having fish flying in and out of me branches instead of birds."

"Frank. That's enough. You're going to wear yourself out thinking about it."

"And if I was a butternut tree I'd rather be a dead stump than to see my nuts all shriveled up and eternally pickled in river water instead of being tugged at and nuzzled by a nice family of squirrels!"

"Frank! Don't listen to him, Mary Ann Alice!"

"And if I was a tamarack…"

"Enough!"

The other day, Mickey McGuire Jr. told me something that his Great-uncle Ronald told him about old Jack McCafferty's rock.

Years and years ago there was a rock at McCafferty's shore half on the water about the size of a big load of hay. When Jack was a little boy he used to climb up on it and lie down there and think about what he'd be doing when he grew up. About what he'd be like. Would he be big and strong and handsome and happy and honest and rich?

The rock had a crack right down the middle about as wide as his young fist.

He would lie there and put his ear on the crack and listen to the mystery down there and the gurgling water far, far down and sometimes a grand beautiful big water spider would peek up to see what was going on and then duck back down quick as lightning.

Every year the crack got wider because of the winter ice. The older Jack got, the wider the crack. The crack became a gap. The gap became a fault.

Every spring Jack would go down to the rock, climb up and jump across the fault.

The older he got, the weaker he got and the wider the space in the rock got and the harder it was to jump until one spring he was too old and the fault was too wide and he couldn't jump it.

Now that rock is two rocks and old Jack is an old man waiting to die.

The rock is like a clock for him.

The clock of his life...

And the river will soon cover it forever...

That Mickey.

Maybe he has the soul of a poet, too.

3

The Only One

A MONTH of Miss Fish is just about enough for me. She's making us memorize dates now. In 4004 B.C. God created heaven and earth. In 3875 B.C. Adam and Eve had a son named Cain and a year later, another kid named Abel. By 3679 B.C. there were lots of people in the world. All of them doing dirty, filthy, sinful things that we can't talk about. In 2349 B.C. Noah built an ark and put all the animals on it and shoved his wife kicking and screaming on it and sailed away during the flood and everybody d— except Noah and what's her name his wife and all the animals.

That kind of thing.

We had a test the other day. First question: "What happened in the year 4004 B.C.?"

My answer: "Thousands of Paleo Indians are living in Canada in tents made of saplings and animal skins. They eat meat and berries. The young women wear short leather skirts to show off their tattoos!"

Second question: "What happened in 2349 B.C.?"

My answer: "First library built in Egypt. Skiing invented in Norway. Birch-bark canoes plentiful on the rivers in Canada. The rivers are like highways. The canoes are like cars except they don't have wheels and a horn."

All stuff we learned from Patchy.

I got another F.

I think I'll quit school.

Doobie Noonan did.

"You're a strange one, Miss Fishy," she up and says one day to Miss Fish, and walks out. Working full time at the dam site now. Now she sees Andy Ryan every day. But he doesn't see her.

I'm only working part time.

Won't be long, though, till nobody's working at the dam site. The dam's almost finished.

Only a few weeks left.

Andy Ryan has made over a hundred dangerous trips with his team across the top of the dam. He's a hero. He's famous all up and down the river. Everybody loves Andy.

Poor Doobie.

I told Miss Fish I had a three-hundred-million-year-old dragonfly at home. I asked if she'd like me to bring it in and do a bit of a talk about it to the class.

She said if I didn't change my attitude I was headed for a life full of trouble and sorrow.

The Corks row down the river now almost every day looking for mail from the little lawyer that they'll never get. My father tries to tell them every day that they're never going to get any kind of message from the little weasel and that they'd better get ready to move because they're going to be flooded out.

The Corks won't listen.

My father is still trying to raise money along the river to help the Corks get another place but nobody has very much money and some of them are saying that even if they did have some extra money they wouldn't give it to the Corks anyway because the Corks are too stubborn and stupid and don't deserve any help. People won't help people who won't help themselves, they say. Some say squatters they are and squatters they'll remain.

My father told Mr. Cork that he was arranging to get some money together to help them move before the water came up but Mr. Cork got mad and stuck out his chin and said he'd rather drown than accept one red cent from anybody and that's it!

"I'm not movin'. That's my home and I'm stayin' in it!"

And another thing about the Corks.

They're also fishing around for other gossip. Gossip and news about the dam. About the new teacher. About Mrs. Drizzle. And Patchy. And Patchy's boat. And did they find anything else? And what are people saying about what happened to Patchy? Do they all say he's gone forever?

What does Father Foley say? Is there going to be a funeral?

The Corks have never asked so many questions before. They never used to care what anybody else thought.

Never cared what the rest of the world was doing.

I look straight at Mr. and Mrs. Cork.

"I don't believe what they're all saying about Patchy Drizzle," I say to them. Both of them have their clay pipes between their teeth.

"You don't?" they both say.

"No, I don't," I say.

"Are you the only one, then?" says Mr. Cork.

"Looks like it," I say.

4

The Gray Phantom

ANDY Ryan is getting so rich, what with being paid the sixty cents an hour for himself and his wonderful team of horses. Sixty cents an hour is six dollars a day is thirty-six dollars a week is one hundred and forty-four dollars a month is one thousand seven hundred twenty-eight dollars a year! Nobody around here has ever seen that much money.

Now, listen to this, will ya?

Andy Ryan's gone and bought himself a radio! He's the only one in the whole township, as far as I know, who has a radio. They're the big rage in New York City, they say.

And not only that.

Andy Ryan has finally noticed Doobie Noonan. Not only has he noticed her but now hasn't he asked her to go over to his place this coming Sunday to help him listen to his radio, if you please!

Doobie says she heard that they play grand dance

music over the radio. She says maybe Andy Ryan will ask her to dance while the radio is playing.

I start to tease her a bit.

"Maybe, Doobie, while the radio is playing away, he'll get down on his knee and ask you to marry him!"

By the look on her face I know she takes me serious. She doesn't think it's a joke at all.

"Maybe he will," she says.

"Doobie, he's away too old for you. He's nineteen, isn't he? Goin' on twenty?"

"That's nothing," says Doobie. "The Gray Phantom, that Lovable Outlaw, is right now fiddlin' with a female only half his age!"

I guess they'll go to his place after church on Sunday. There's a special requiem service for Mr. Peter Drizzle. Father Foley says enough time is passed and it's now appropriate to say good-bye to Patchy. They'll have a funeral service but no burial.

The Mass for the Dead will be said.

And Mary Ann Alice will ring soft for Patchy.

There'll be one person there, though, who will think this mass is unnecessary.

5

No Chickadees

I T ' S Sunday and the church is jammed for Patchy's funeral mass. They're standing outside listening at the windows and around the door. Many of my hundred lads from mess hall number one are here. Lots of them stayed over special to go. They would usually go home to their own villages on Sunday. It seems odd and a bit funny to see some of them dressed in Sunday clothes instead of dressed in cement. Their suits are either too big or too small.

Lannigan's is too small for him. His collar is choking him and his arms are hanging way down out of the sleeves of his coat. The pants look like he borrowed them from some kid or other.

Father Foley says a remembrance about Patchy.

He was a wonderful teacher, he says. He says Patchy had his own scientific ideas about the world and he was entitled to them. He says that God gave us minds and it's good to use them and that there was nobody like Patchy to get you to use your mind. Investigating and questioning is good, Father Foley says, as long as you have faith and follow the teachings of the greatest teacher of all, Our Lord Jesus Christ. And also Father Foley forgives Patchy Drizzle for taking the sacrament of marriage in a church not of our faith. Amen. I'm wishing there was a few chickadees flying around in here to help Father Foley out.

Communion takes forever because there's so many people. I notice the first ones up in the line to receive the host are Andy Ryan and Doobie Noonan.

I've lent Doobie my green outfit for this occasion. She's developed about the same way I have and so the clothes fit her just right. She's a bit taller than me though, so the skirt is a bit shorter.

Mickey McGuire Jr. is in the line with me.

"Look," he says, "there goes Doobie Noonan with Andy Ryan. And look, aren't those your blue clothes she's wearin'?"

"Green, Mickey," I say. "Say green or I'll take out my hammer after ya!"

"Green," says Mickey. "I meant green."

Even the Corks are here today, to say good-bye to Patchy. Mr. and Mrs. Cork and the kids, Balder and Rowan.

The Corks are dressed the best they can and nobody stares at them. Mr. Cork is wearing an old worn-out suit that must belong to Grampa Cork. Mrs. Cork's dress is made of rough-looking material and dyed. The kids are clean but their shirts don't fit right. And their hair is stuck down with something. Probably bear grease.

Nobody looks at the Cork family's feet. What they're wearing.

The Cork family are all wearing gum rubbers instead of shoes. Nobody laughs at them. Nobody's cruel.

Mr. Cork doesn't take communion. He slips outside with some of the other men and smokes his pipe.

And at the back of the church, where nobody notices except me, there's Mrs. Victoria Drizzle.

From Wakefield, England, here at her husband's funeral in Martindale, Canada.

All alone.

6
Off to Wakefield

THIS week, the week after the funeral, everything seems to be happening at once.

The cement for the main dam is finished. The steel gates for the Spillway are almost ready to be put in. The coffer dam is moved over in front of the By-Pass and the Cement Heads are plugging the By-Pass with concrete. Now the river is dumping through the dam through the pipes and generators.

The Paugan Falls is now a huge cement wall with pipes coming through a brick building with generators inside that will make electricity once it's all set.

Soon everything will get shut and the water will pile up.

There aren't a hundred lads in mess hall number one anymore. Every day there's less and less lads. There's less and less cement.

And there's more food for Lannigan. He's still here. He's staying till the last, he says.

On Monday, the day after Patchy's funeral, Mrs. Victoria Drizzle put a For Sale sign up in front of the little white house.

I went to see her.

"Mary Ann Alice," she said, "Peter put this house in my name. Now I'm going to sell it and if I do I'll have enough resources to travel back home to Wakefield, England. I want to tell you something from my heart," she said. "I want to tell you that you are the one person I will miss when I'm gone. I will write down my address for you and you must write to me and I will write to you. You are an intelligent, brave and beautiful girl and I have benefited greatly from having met you."

It was quite a mouthful.

She had wet eyes when she said it.

I waited for her to say something about Patchy but she didn't say a word about him.

On Tuesday, the day after the For Sale sign went up, the big chief engineer himself bought the house.

"I told you," my father said. "He loves it around here. He's going to use the house as a summer place. He'll come up here on his holidays and arrange to marry both of the O'Malley girls at once. I have it on good authority. Father Foley told me in strict confidence and to keep it a secret but I don't mind tellin' you, darlin'."

Mrs. Drizzle told me that the big chief engineer in charge of the dam came right over to the house in his funny clothes and started pulling money out of his pockets until there was enough.

Then she said this: "Mr. Drizzle is gone, my dear. We have to accept that. You have to accept that."

I looked at her.

I looked at her but I didn't agree with her. I didn't accept that.

"I want you to take his rock collection. And his tools. I know he'd want you to have them. They're out in the back. You arrange with the big chief engineer himself, as they call him, to make sure you get them before he takes over the house."

"What are you going to do?" I said.

"I'm taking the train to Ottawa on Friday. Then I'm taking the train to Montreal on Saturday. In Montreal I'm taking an ocean liner to England. To where I belong. And I'm never coming back."

On Thursday just about all the lads are gone from the cement job and only Lannigan and a few others are left to finish it all off.

"I wonder what we're going to do with all this food we're left with?" says Mrs. Kealey. "I don't suppose Lannigan would eat it all for us do, do you think? Save us throwing it out."

On Friday Mrs. Drizzle takes the morning train. There are other people on the platform but I'm the only one there to see her off.

I wrote a poem once about trains. The poem wasn't one of my best but Patchy said the ideas in it were good. The poem said that trains can be exciting or sad. If you're getting on one yourself, it's exciting. If somebody else is getting on and you're not, it's sad.

She's all dressed up with a dark suit with a tight jacket and a small pillbox hat. She looks pretty nice and tidy. She has one small suitcase with her.

She gets up on the step the conductor puts down for her and takes off her glove and puts out her hand to me.

"Good-bye," she says, "Mary Ann Alice. I will tell them very proudly at home when I get there that I met a very unique young lady who is named after a sacred church bell!"

"Thank you," I say. "I hope you can be happy."

She turns and steps up into the car. She doesn't wave. She doesn't look back.

I try to see what seat she takes but I can't. The morning sun is blinding the windows. All you can see in the windows is the reflection of us standing on the platform. People are waving but not at her. I wave a little, too. I wonder if she's looking.

The train grunts and then slides away. Not far from the station the train curves into the bush and disappears. The whistle gives a lonesome toot. Now all that's left is floating smoke. All that's left of Mrs. Drizzle.

On Saturday the cement is finished. At noon for dinner, my hundred lads are down to a half a dozen. There's only me and Mrs. Kealey working.

Lannigan comes in and says he's sad that the cement is all over and he says he thinks he's not hungry.

"Not hungry?" says Mrs. Kealey to me. "Watch this!" Lannigan sits down and looks around. He's looking bigger than ever.

He drinks up a pitcher of cream and sits back. Mrs. Kealey puts a roast of beef in front of him and a bowl of boiled potatoes that would feed a whole table. He gets a stack of green onions and a soup bowl of salt. He has a tray of butter. He has his own table.

The other half-dozen lads have their own table.

Lannigan is playing with his food.

Mrs. Kealey comes down with her spoon.

"I went to a lot of trouble preparing this grub for you. Now you'll pay me the respect I deserve by digging in and eating every bit of it, me son!"

Then she slams the spoon on the table to get him started. Once he starts there's no stoppin' him. It's Lannigan's last meal with us.

"It's a wonder to behold," says Mrs. Kealey.

"Y'er just like me mother," says Lannigan to Mrs. Kealey. "Always after me to eat more like my three brothers. They eat a lot!"

Mrs. Kealey's mouth drops open. "You have three brothers who eat more than you do?"

"Sure do," says Lannigan. He puts down the big roast of beef he's been gnawing on, just to be polite. For the etiquette of it.

"My mother told me and me brothers never to eat with our mouth full," says Lannigan.

"Don't you mean never to *speak* when your mouth is full?" says Mrs. Kealey.

"Oh, yeah. That's right. I got it wrong." He picks up the roast beef and chaws about a pound of it off into his gob.

"Never *speak* wif yer mouf foe—not never *eat* wif yer mouf foe."

"We're going to miss Lannigan," says Mrs. Kealey. "And I'm going to pray for his mother."

7

Closed

THEY closed the dam this morning. It's starting.

We're all waiting for the water to come up.

My father has dug a line halfway up our lower field where we think the water will stop.

I'm standing down by our wharf looking at the empty space where Patchy used to tie up his boat.

I'm starting to think maybe they're right. Maybe Patchy is gone forever. But why did they never find him? They combed the shores. They dove in the water. They searched the caves. No Patchy.

And his geology bag. Why was it empty? Where were his tools and his bottles of chemicals and his samples? Why would he empty the bag and then get into his boat?

I can't understand it. It doesn't make any sense.

But still, I'm starting to give up. Specially today.

It's so quiet here this morning I can hear myself breathing.

Now I hear something else.

One, two, three, squeak! And then the bailing can scraping the boat. One, two, three, squeak. Bail.

Soon around the point come the Corks.

They tie up their boat.

We stand on the wharf watching the water. It seems more still than usual. Standing quiet. I can see a pickerel down there. Facing upstream. Not moving. Is he waiting, too?

The Corks want all the news. Mrs. Cork's clay pipe is broken. She's holding it together to smoke it. "Busted me dudeen with the bailing can," she says.

I give them all the news. Doobie Noonan's listening to the radio with Andy Ryan who's too old for her. The dam is finished and shut. The water will start to come up today.

"Not up at our place it won't," says Mr. Cork. He bites his clay pipe and sticks out his chin.

The cement gang is all gone and Lannigan has three brothers who eat more than he does and Mrs. Kealey is going to pray for their mother.

What else? Oh, yes. No, there's no letter from no lawyer or anybody else.

What else? Oh, yes. The big chief engineer with the funny clothes bought Patchy Drizzle's house from Mrs. Victoria Wakefield Drizzle.

What else? Oh, yes.

Mrs. Drizzle's gone. Forever.

Gone back home to Wakefield, England.

"Gone, is she?" says Mrs. Cork.

"Well, that's a bit of good news, isn't it?" says Mr. Cork.

"What's good about it?" I say. My head's starting to heat up.

"Well, she never much liked anybody or anything around here anyway, did she?" says Mrs. Cork.

My father walks onto the wharf.

"Well, what's it going to be, Mr. Cork?" he says. "Today's the day. Are you gonna clear out or not?"

"I'm not," says Mr. Cork. His chin is out so far he's in danger of swallowing his dudeen.

"Well, don't say we didn't try to warn ya!" my father says.

After a while the Corks get back in their boat and squeak and bail up the river and around the point and out of sight.

"There's nothing more anybody can do for them," my father says.

"What's going to happen to them?" I say.

"God only knows," says my father. "I'll tell you one thing though, Mary Ann Alice. They'd better get themselves a few more bailing cans because they're gonna be bailin' out more than their boat before this is over!"

The rest of the day we spend taking apart the wharf and carrying the boards up to just above the spot in the middle of our lower field where my father dug the trench mark where he thinks the water will rise to.

Then we get the team and harness them up and skid the two big booms that float the wharf up to the mark, too.

All the time we watch the river, stare at the water. But

it's not moving. It's very still. It's thinking about it.

I'm almost hypnotized sometimes, watching it so hard. It hasn't come up one inch.

Then we get the horses to drag our big rowboat out of the water and up the long slope to above the marker and tie it there to a stake in the ground.

It looks lonesome up there, our boat does, on dry land like that. High as two church steeples' worth, right, Patchy?

Then we put our wharf back together.

At supper at the table we eat without looking at our food. We look out the window down at the river sitting there. Sometimes I look down at my farmer and his wife and the person in the rowboat on the tablecloth.

After supper my father goes down to the shore and blows his bugle for a while. My mother and I sit in the swing in the yard and watch the river.

"I fell in love with your father because of that bugle," my mother says.

"Is that the way you fall in love?" I say.

"It's as good a way as any," my mother says.

"I wonder how I'll go about it," I say.

"Plenty of time for that," my mother says. "Don't be in a mad rush. Like Doobie."

After the bugle stops and the echo of the bugle off the mountain drifts away and my father comes back up and stands beside us in the yard we are wrapped in quiet.

I've never heard it as quiet.

Not a breeze in the pines. Not the flutter of a bird's

wing. Not the scratch of a chicken. Not a cricket. Not the buzz of a fly. Not the crack of a twig.

Are we holding our breath? Is the river holding its breath?

When it's about dark we go in and light the lamps and have a cuppa tea.

"We'll try to get some sleep," my mother says. "See what tomorrow brings."

On the way to bed my father tries to cheer me up. "Father Foley told me the other day in all confidence that God told Noah to bring his wife along because He knew that the ark would be leakin' like a sieve and Noah would need somebody to bail. Keep bailing, woman! Noah kept yelling."

The joke falls away. I give my father a kiss and go up to bed.

I blow out my lamp and to take my mind off the river I try to imagine what it will be like when we get the electricity.

8

Here Comes Everybody

IN my dream I'm serving a mob in a mess hall that looks a lot like mess hall number one. The noise of everybody eating would deafen ya! I'm all alone serving. Mrs. Kealey is in the cookhouse cooking everything all at once—breakfast, dinner and supper. Lannigan and all the lads are there. Everybody's yelling for more and sponging the sweat off their heads.

I run from table to table throwing down the platters and bowls of everything. Then I run back for more. They're pounding the tables with the forks and knives in their fists. They're chanting, "Mary Ann Alice! Mary Ann Alice!"

Mrs. Kealey roars out of the heat of the kitchen and smashes a lot of them over the head with a wooden spoon the size of a log.

Miss Fish is there, sitting across from Lannigan. She's filling her face with beans and porridge and cabbage. Lannigan reaches over and dumps a pitcher of buttermilk over her head. She growls at him and shows her teeth like a poisoned dog.

Mean Hughie is at a table of his own. He's got a big fork and a carving knife. Lying on the table in front of him is William Davenport, the little lawyer. Mean Hughie is carving slices off him and stuffing them into W.D.'s shiny leather briefcase.

Everybody's mopping sweat and chanting and gobbling like pigs and wolves.

Prime Minister Mackenzie King is drinking pea soup out of his hat.

The O'Malley girls are feeding the big chief engineer himself tablespoons and soup ladles of lard out of a barrel.

Andy Ryan is leading his team of horses around the mess hall. The horses have their snouts in bags of flour tied round their heads. Doobie Noonan is riding one of them. She has no clothes on except for a hat. The hat is a cabbage.

Mrs. Victoria Drizzle is throwing hard-boiled eggs at Lannigan's head.

Fuzzy and Frank McCrank are having a stack of bread and butter and a pail of tea with the farmer and the farmer's wife from the tablecloth. Is the person in the rowboat with them? Who is it?

Mr. Kealey is up to his waist in stew.

Mrs. McSorley has a little sign hanging around baby Ambrose's neck. The sign says, "What am I?"

Mr. McLaughlan is sitting with Algonquin Art. They're slapping the table with pancakes and syrup and laughing their heads off. Jackie Boyle's in his coffin surrounded by his big family all eating pork and bean sandwiches.

The Corks are pouring maple syrup into Grampa Cork's spit pail. There's cats sticking out of their pockets.

I'm yellin' at them that I have the soul of a poet but nobody wants to listen. Just keep the food comin' Mary Ann Alice!

Great-uncle Ronald and Mickey McGuire Jr. and that whole gang are all gnawing on pigs' feet. Mayor Even Steven is stuffing his pockets with bacon. Mickey is wearing my green outfit.

The McCooeys are all fighting over a giant roast beef in the corner. Now they're eating rocks.

There's pork hocks with wings soaring around like hawks.

Old Jack McCafferty is climbing into the fault in his rock.

Eddy and Lizzie Lamarr, Fitzpatrick the ferryman, Noah and what's her name his wife are in the ark. Also in the ark is Father Foley. He has nuthatches and chickadees sitting on his head. Father Foley is chanting, "Bail! Bail! Bail!"

At the end of the main table is sitting Arthur the Arthropod. He's bigger than everybody. Even bigger than Lannigan. He's eating everything. There's fire coming out of his mouth. His transparent wings are fanning up and down. He belches.

Hold on! Who's that just slipped out the door into the sound of war? Somebody we know! Hey, you! Wait a minute! Come back here! I see you! You can't run away from me! I know who you are! Turn around! Turn around and let me see your face. Turn around! I'm screaming. I have you by the arm. Turn. There's water everywhere.

"Turn around!"

I'm sitting up in bed in the dark. I'm soaked in sweat. I can hear myself crying out, "Turn around! I know it's you!"

I hear my mother outside my room and see her flickering lamp under the door. The door opens and the yellow lamplight knifes in.

"My God, Mary Ann Alice, have ya seen a ghost, or what?"

"I think I have, Mother," I say. "But it's all right. Only a dream. I thought I saw you know who. I chased him but he wouldn't turn around so I could see his face!"

"Oh, my dear Mary Ann Alice. Look at the time. It's almost light. Yer father's sound asleep. Put on yer clothes. We'll walk down careful and see where the water is. You have to let Patchy go. Once the water's up, it'll be over. You'll know for sure then."

Soon as we get outside we can hear it.

There's a gurgling, whirling kind of soft roar.

It's hard to see because it's only just barely coming to dawn.

Down part way we stop to hear a flowing rush like a big tub emptying. I look back at our kitchen window flickering with the lamp. If you can see your kitchen window, you're safe.

We sit beside the rebuilt wharf and our boat where they are at my father's mark.

And we wait.

By the middle of the morning the river is breathing in and out and coming up higher with each breath.

By noon there is so much broken junk floating it's hard to see the water.

By afternoon the stuff floating isn't as thick. But there's a lot of broken trees. You can tell what the water is doing. Even though the river is still coming up, it's still flowing. There's still a current.

"They must be letting some of the top water through the Spillway gates," my father says.

By supper time the water is up to where our wharf and boat are.

Now the wharf is floating. Will the water stop?

Now the boat is floating.

And now, after an hour or so, it looks like my father was exactly right. The river has stopped rising right where he said it would.

Our river is now three times as wide as it was. And everything—the mountain, the point, the shore—looks so strange.

And out there, coming in view past the point, what's that big thing floating there? Half sunk. Boards. Windows. A tin roof. A chimney.

It's a house!

"It's the Cork house!" my father yells. "It's the Cork house!"

We pile in our big rowboat and fight our way through the brush and broken trees floating.

The Cork house is half sunk but floating pretty straight up. The second floor is above water. Through the bedroom window we can see somebody moving. Closer now.

Mr. Cork leans out the window.

"Gidday!" says Mr. Cork through his teeth, biting his dudeen.

I stand up in the boat and grab the window sill and lean in to see.

They've moved Grampa Cork's bed upstairs.

"Grampa Cork's dead!" Mrs. Cork says. "Died last night." The two kids Rowan and Balder are over at the opposite window, looking out. There are cats all over the place. It's gloomy in there. Hard to see.

There's another person in the room over by the far wall.

Sometimes I think of something and all of a sudden it comes true. It happened last Christmas near the church before I saw Mrs. Drizzle.

Right now I'm thinking of something but I'm afraid to say it, even to myself.

The figure moves forward toward me into the light. I can see him now coming toward me. Tall, wide shoulders, on the skinny side, sticky-out ears. Now the sandy hair and the blue eyes.

I can't breathe. Yes! It is!

It's Patchy Drizzle!

9

Two Rivers

WHAT used to be little valleys along the river where we'd pick berries are now inlets full of river.

What used to be faces of rock on the side of the mountain are now walls that drop right into the water.

What used to be farmers' fields are now big deep bays. What used to be rapids is now flat calm water. What used to be little whirlpools is now flat calm water. What used to be small falls is now flat calm water. What used to be a big waterfall is now a dam.

What used to be a mountain is now only part of a mountain.

Mickey McGuire Jr. is rowing.

It's easy rowing upriver now because there's almost no current. Floating along this way now feels like flying. I still feel the real river way down underneath me.

We're rowing up to see what the river is like now where the Cork farm used to be.

Where Patchy Drizzle hid and pretended to be dead.

"I'm sorry, Mary Ann Alice," Patchy said to me. "It was the only way Victoria would ever go back home to Wakefield, England, where she belongs."

Patchy was planning how to be dead but not dead ever since he found Arthur the Arthropod. A bit like Arthur when you think about it. Dead but not dead.

Patchy was in the caves when the explosion went off. All of a sudden he said he could see how his plan would work. He emptied his geology bag and wrapped the stuff in his shirt. Then, in the smoke and confusion, he left the empty bag for people to find (he hoped I would wonder why the bag was empty).

Then he shoved his boat out into the fast water around the coffer dam and let it be sucked down the By-Pass.

Then he crawled along the cliff base to calmer water, tied his shirt around his neck and swam to the other side.

It took him two days to walk up the river through the bush to the Cork farm.

The night he spent with the black flies on the mountain made him sick but Mrs. Cork nursed him better. The Corks kept him caught up with all the gossip.

He stayed with the stubborn Corks while the river came up. His plan was they'd all take off in their boat when the water got high enough but by the time Mr. Cork was ready to give up, the leaky boat was lost in the flood and they were stranded. Patchy made them stay in the house. He said the house was like Noah's Ark.

"Did Victoria say anything personal about me when

you saw her off on the train?" Patchy asked me.

Out of my mouth came a lie.

"Yes," I said. "She did."

"What did she say?"

Out of my mouth came another lie.

"She said you were a kind and decent man."

What people don't know won't hurt them, I always say.

Mickey McGuire Jr. is rowing smooth and easy along. We're flying two church steeples above the old river. One river on top of another river. A modern river on top of an ancient river forever.

It's hard to spot where the Cork farm was, everything is so changed. It's a whole new world here.

All of a sudden I realize that I'm looking right at it. The top of the cliff that was behind the Cork farm. The cliff that we stood on that was like the prow of a big ocean liner. It was that high.

Only now it's only about one oar length high. You could sit on the edge and dangle your feet over and nearly touch the water.

We pull the boat along the side and scramble up to the ledge.

I look down into the water at my feet. It's black down there. Straight down there where the farm used to be.

The other evening I was on the swing with Mickey McGuire Jr. and my mother and father were on the porch and we're all watching the new river sit there like a big lake. I touched Mickey's back and it felt as hard as a wall of rock.

Mickey's hair is straight and black. Every so often he'll run his fingers across it to keep it from falling over his eyes. Or he'll toss his head to throw his hair back. His ears are perfect, shaped just right and close to his head. His coat lies easy across his chest and loose on his lumpy shoulders and I already told you about his hands when he rows the boat.

He has cheek bones that you can see and his jaw cuts down along his chin. He's got a crease on the left side of his cheek when he smiles. His nose is strong on his face.

His eyes are brown. He has long eyelashes.

He looks away sometimes when he's talking to you and then he looks back right at you, like your dog would, head on the side. Trusting you.

When he's thinking hard he bites his lips.

He smells clean and warm and deep, like the granary.

His voice is big, even when he's whispering.

"Gawd, it's so quiet, Mary Ann Alice," he whispers loud. I have to smile at his whispering.

When he's embarrassed or afraid or excited he swallows, and his Adam's apple runs up and down his throat.

He's swallowing now. Up then down goes the Adam's apple.

His lips look like they've been carved by an artist.

My hand feels soft inside his hard hand.

On the horizon I can see the steeple of St. Martin's Church.

And now I can hear the sad and muffled bell that tolls for Grampa Cork.

Mary Ann Alice, Mary Ann Alice.
It's time to kiss Mickey McGuire Jr.
Mickey's afraid but it's all right. Our lips touch.
I'm kissing him but not only him.
I'm also kissing my lovely Gatineau River good-bye.

Epilogue

When I get sad, afraid or feeling low
And start to hang my head and sulk and pine
And stack up all my sorrows in a row
Like sheaves of grain in stooks along the line;
Or, say I think I have a broken heart
Because of something someone said to me
That poured a dam against my flowing art,
And made me think of what I'd never be.
    That is when I turn my thoughts to you
    My River Gatineau! The way you were
    So full of joy and trickery! You who
    Used to jump and run and hide and purr!
        And so I can, by scribbling with this pen,
        As if by magic, be myself again!

Mary Ann Alice McCrank (poet)

Author's Note

The Paugan Dam at Low, Quebec on the Gatineau River was, at the time of its completion in 1928, "one of the major power plants of the world."[1] It was soon eclipsed in size and output by the great dams built since that time but that does not minimize the impact that the project at Low had on the isolated people of the countryside there.

It wasn't until two generations later that local people got electric power and proper deeds to what remained of the land they'd cleared with their horses, axes and saws. One deed, in fact, was not officially obtained until 1998, just months before the international corporation's ninety-nine-year lease ran out.

I have telescoped the actual time it took to complete the dam to suit my narration. The water rose in the spring of 1928, not the previous fall. And it took much longer.

Poetic license courtesy of Mary Ann Alice McCrank.

All other background historical detail is, to my best knowledge and efforts, accurate.

—Brian Doyle

[1] *The Canadian Engineer*, Feb 21, 1928, Vol. 54, No. 8. p225.